Games Without Frontiers
By Matt Turney

"There are no facts, only interpretations."
Friedrich Nietzsche

for Layla and Maci, may all your dreams in life come true

A legend will always live longer than the truth.

1.

Sept '90s

Paul casually yawns himself awake and stretches his hand over to the alarm clock that is basically lying on his head. He slaps the wake button just enough to make the alarm quit sounding and then opens and closes his eyes as he scratches the back of his head. Paul stands up and falls right back to the bed. No strength in his legs yet. Still trying to stand, he falls safely back into the bed and underneath the covers. His head is pounding. The previous evening he had been celebrating the night with his buddies. Lots of drinking had been involved. Before Paul even arrived at the party, he'd made a stop for his own bottle of whiskey.

The Whiskey bottle was already empty and sitting over in the corner of his room. Paul turns his head up to look at the empty bottle sitting on the counter of the desk.

Games Without Frontiers

"What was I thinking?" Paul says aloud. "Jesus Christ." Then a huge yawn takes over control of his entire body as he moves around the bed, trying to stretch out but also to continue to stay warm under the blanket.

Not much movement is involved, and there Paul sits, wrapped up in a literal nutshell. "Okay, time to get up."

Sitting up on the side of his bed, Paul looks into a mirror with his reflection staring right back at him. He stands, bends over, and walks ever so slightly to the mirror, scratching his would-be chin-hair that, after three weeks of careful growing, was still merely peach fuzz on his chin. Then stretching some more and yawning some more, he looks down at his cell phone. Two texts: one is from Lindsey; the other is from FMooth. The Lindsey message says, "Call me <3 <3 Lyns, =)". It was sent at 1:07 a.m. The FMooth message says, "Where the hell r u, we getting grub" at 3:33 a.m. Paul plays the previous night around in his head, noticing how hung-over he feels.

After Paul is fully dressed he heads out of his room and walks down the hallway of his parents house. Entering into the bathroom and shutting the door behind him, he thinks, *What the hell was I doing at three?* FMooth was a friend Paul had known forever and it was unlikely that he would have purposely ditched one of his friends. "What was I doing at three?" Paul says aloud.

"I was with Lindsey at the party, and I know I dropped her off at home, but where did I go instead of the party."

A loud beeping, buzzing sound starts blaring from Paul's phone, which is still in his bedroom. Paul finishes washing his face, dries it, and then sprints from the bathroom back to his room through the hallway. The phone is on its fourth and last ring as Paul leans down and picks it up of the floor. He quickly reads the phone display to see that the call is coming from a friend of his: Shelly. He smiles as he presses "enter" and holds it up to his ear.

"Wassup," Paul yells loudly and kinda crazily.

"How are you? Hangover?" says the soft voice of Shelly on the other end. She giggles slightly after the question.

"Hungover? Nope. Why would I be hungover?" he giggles back into the phone line and then lets out a deep breath.

"Yeah, what the fuck ever. You were acting kinda crazy last night."

"How was I being crazy?"

"You were just acting strange. Just acting a little weird."

"I don't even remember coming home last night. How did I get home?"

"I brought you home. You don't remember that?"

"I don't remember what?"

Theres a long pause. Paul doesn't say anything, because he can't think of anything to say.

Games Without Frontiers

Nothing on the other end of the line either, but he can hear Shelly's light breath get a little stronger. Then a little sound echoes through the phone from her end that sounds like a stuffy nose. The cellphones scratches out a couple of light small pops, then a shuddery light whisper, "It's okay, I don't … I just thought that the way you were acting, that you liked me."

"I do like you."

"You know what I mean?"

"Look, I got a girlfriend."

Shelly hangs up on him. Paul looks down at the phone. The duration of the conversation was almost ten minutes. It felt like much shorter, and much longer, at the same time. Paul shuffles through the numbers in his phone log till the number highlights Lindsey and presses "send."

The phone rings, and while it rings, Paul starts to think, *It would probably be best if she doesn't talk to me right now, so I hope she doesn't pick up.* Luckily, the phone rings till the voicemail. "This is Lindsey. Leave a message, and if this is Paul, I love you lots."

"Hey it's me, just trying to call." Slight pause. "Guess I'll talk to you later. Love ya."

If Paul had done anything the night before with someone else that Lindsey would find out about, she most likely would have answered the phone and been furious. So she didn't know anything.

The phone buzzes and vibrates in his hand: incoming, Shelly.

Paul hits end and throws the phone down on his bed. He decides to check his schedule at the restaurant where he works. He had to be in at six that evening, "Well, shit." Thinking about the fact he had to work later that day seemed even worse when he looks at the clock and it's three-thirty.

While debating on whether to work out or take the day off, his phone began to ring. Paul looks to see that it is Richard, a co-worker and the host of the party he attended last night.

"Wassup."

"Wassup."

"Nothing."

"Everything turn out all right last night? You seemed pissed when you left."

"I don't really remember anything."

"Oh really, pimp, you don't remember trying to act like you were drunk, so hard?"

"I wasn't acting. I feel like shit today."

"Yeah, one of the reasons I called is because you gave me your wallet for some reason, and I still have it."

Paul looks around his room profoundly. "Oh shit, dude, I didn't even know it was gone."

"Yeah, I've got it, and I just wanted to call and let you know I didn't steal it, and it stills has all its money in it, but Sam took the condoms out of it."

Games Without Frontiers

"Fucker. Well, thanks man, you saved me a lot of worrying, I'm sure."

"It's cool, yeah. Shelly started getting all over you after Lindsey left, and you told me to hold your wallet so she wouldn't try and steal it."

"Ha-ha-ha." Laughs on both ends of the phone line.

"Well, I'm not really sure what happened between me and Shelly, but she's already called here sounding upset."

"Don't worry, dude, you were trying everything to keep her off of you, and she wouldn't let up."

They both pause.

"You ended up leaving with her. Through all the struggle, I just kept telling her you could stay at the house with me."

"At least I had enough sense to hide my money. Shady bitch."

"Dude gotta run. I'll get your wallet back to you later." Click on the telephone line, and end.

Paul decides just to chill until work. Sitting in his desk chair, he begins to think, *Maybe I didn't do anything last night.*

The phone rings and begins to vibrate again. He hopes for Lindsey, but it's Shelly. Hesitating over whether to press "answer" or "end," he looks at himself once again in the mirror and stares at himself. Paul raises the phone and puts it to his ear, "Hello?"

"Look, you said a lot of things last night ..."

Paul interrupts. "I don't remember saying anything." Very soulless and dry.

"It's just, I really like you, and I know you have a girlfriend, it just hurts to think."

He interrupts once again."Well then, don't think about it."

"Look, you don't have to be a dick."

"I'm not being anyway. It's just that you're trying to make this sound as if you and me are something we're not."

"I know, I just can't …"

"Can't what?"

"It's just I really like you …"

"I don't care, said Pierre, I'm from France." Paul hangs the phone up.

Later in the day, although happy to have his wallet back, the Roadhouse Restaurant shift drags by exceptionally slowly that evening. All Paul can do is think about getting out of there, even considering quitting his job at any moment if something upsets him.

When he gets off work, Paul walks out to his car, opens the door, gets in, and reaches to the cup holder where his cellphone is.

Paul checks his call log, and is a little surprised that he hasn't received any missed calls. Strange. Paul would usually always have a message of some sort, at least from Lindsey. But there was nothing, so he calls her anyway.

Games Without Frontiers

"Hello," Lindsey answers in a very quiet tone.

"Hey, is everything okay?"

"Yeah, yeah." She quickly responds, her pitch a little louder. "It's just, something happened earlier, and I really don't know how to feel about it."

"What happened?" Paul asks.

"You know that girl that we go to school with, Shelly Summers?"

"Yeah, I guess so."

"Apparently she was acting really strange around everyone today, and she got into a car and got extremely drunk, and she was driving around. At some point she passed out behind the wheel and ran off the side of the road."

"Is she okay?" Paul asks, not quite sure what emotion to feel.

"Apparently, she died on impact. Killed her instantly."

"No way." Paul is genuinely shocked. The phone drops right out of his palm and hits the floor mat of the driver seat. Paul can hear Lindsey's voice echoing from the phone on the gound. "Are you okay, Paul? Paul?"

His hand begins shaking, and he decides not to reach for the phone on the floorboard. In no way did Paul know that he would be forever changed after this day. Still frozen, all he can bring himself to do is smoke a cigarette. He loses a little focus on his thoughts and can hear music playing from the car radio very faintly.

Paul reaches for the volume and turns it up.

Its a song he has never heard in his life is playing on the radio.
"Che shoo frontier," it repeats over and over.

From that moment on, anytime anything was ever mentioned
about Shelly, from anyone, the words in that song would be a
reminder blasting into his head. An external sense was now
connected to him at this moment in his life and would be triggered,
without fail, anytime he heard her name or the song.

The cell phone starts to ring again, and all his attention goes
directly to the vibrating floor. The buzzing makes him feel extremely
sick to the stomach. A horrible sickness – the buzzing and vibrating
of the phone continue, and all he can picture is Shelly's face, and all
he can think about is the phone vibrating. For the rest of his life, the
fear and thoughts of a buzzing phone would always make him begin
to feel really sick.

There was much speculation to the sudden death of Shelly
Summers, but nothing was ever confirmed based on any of these
theories. This was a secret Paul would keep to himself for many
years. Walking away from this ordeal with nothing more than a
haunting memory, he decided the best idea would be to let the
situation go. Paul never found out on his own what the words, "Jeux
sans frontiers" meant. One day someone would know the song and
what it meant, but that would be years from now.

2.

Oct '90s

"What are we supposed to do tonight, Ben?" John asks, while staring at the desktop computer and not taking his eyes off the screen for one second. John is typing and clicking away at the computer, which he seems hypnotized by. Ben stands up from the floor where he was comfortably sprawled out all over the place. The two young boys were getting too comfortable and knew that if they didn't decide on plans quickly, they would end up wasting the night away at John's mother's apartment.

"We could go trick-or-treating?" Ben replies sarcastically, but smiling.

"Ha, ha," John responds equally sarcastically, getting more comfortable at his desk.

Ben and John are contemplating what to do this particular evening, because it's their first Halloween with an automobile. John had recently turned 16, and Ben was a good year younger than his best friend. So the two were very excited about this particular holiday, but were yet to have figured out with what to do with this newfound freedom. But here they are,   stuck on a Friday of all nights in John's bedroom with nothing to do, and a license to drive.

Then add the factor its Halloween, and these two young men are about to explode with frustration.

"Why don't we go get a hooker? That could be scary," Ben interjects.

"Are you buying?" John says sharply, sounding off.

"I will if you actually have sex with her, and I get to take a picture of you two."

Ben stands up slowly pacing around the room. "There has got to be something to do, look and see if there are any haunted houses that look interesting. I don't really wanna pay to do anything, 'cause I'm kinda broke."

"Yeah, me too."

"I really don't want to end up spending the night driving, and then maybe stealing a few pumpkins 'cause I have nothing better to do."

And like a crack of a whip, "Hey, this looks good," John exclaims.

Games Without Frontiers

"What is it?" Ben asks.

"Well, I'm looking through this website called "Haunted: Fact or Fiction," and they have all these locations, and there is one about twenty minutes from here!" John becomes more excited with each word.

"I'm listening."

"It's this old cemetery, and apparently it has this kinda big mausoleum in the back, in the oldest part."

"Really?"

"So the legend is that during an outbreak or epidemic of some kind, a whole bunch of the residents in the little town – it's Salem – buried all the children who died in this big-ass mausoleum."

"Whew, now we're talking. So what's the legend say about it?"

"It says the small tomb is about four feet high off the ground, and that if you sit on it,   someone will come up behind you and push you off, like a ghost or spirit."

"I'm sold. Map-quest it."

The two young gentlemen begin preparing for their journey. They grab a couple of flashlights, a six pack of Keystone, a small Swiss army knife, etc.

"Should we bring the video camera?" John asks.

"Nah, we're not making the Blair Witch Project. If it pushes us off and no one believes it, then they can just go fuck themselves," Ben replies.

They gather all of the necessities, and then Ben walks over to the closet opens it up, and reaches down. He comes up with a small billy club bat. "You think we should take this too, just in case?"

"Yeah, sure." John agrees. "Why not? All right, I think that should do it. Let's do it to it."

"HA-HA," Ben raptly retorts. He swings the billy club bat around as if he's attacking the thin air, saying, "That's okay; that's okay," in his best Tony Montana impression. "I kill a pig for fun."

The two skinny, dorky teenagers begin loading up John's 84 Sentra. John pops the trunk, and Ben places their tools in the back. They jump into the front seats.

Their journey has officially begun....

"All I have to say is that those fuckers at Map-quest can kiss my ass. These are the worst fucking directions I've ever seen," Ben exclaims in the passenger seat, scratching his head.

"I'm surprised they don't say turn left at the place where the thing used to be. Then go six-point-two miles, but don't go six-point-three, 'cause that will be too far."

They both laugh as they sit at the gas station getting gas. The two left John's mother's apartment over two hours ago for a trip they imagined would take thirty minutes at the most.

The gas station is a twenty-four-hour Rest Stop, and besides the guy working inside, they are the only ones there.

Games Without Frontiers

"At least it's nice out tonight," John says.

"True … oh shit," Ben's exclaims as his entire demeanor changes and a big red truck pulls into the parking lot, music blaring so loudly no one could understand it if they tried. It was full of fellow classmates from their high school: a few guys and couple of girls. Craig is driving and parks the massive red beast at the front of the Rest Stop, closer to the store itself, and further away from Ben and John. When Craig steps out and down from the lift on his truck, the boys hear nothing but girls and guys yelling in the cab. Craig swings the door and leaves it open as he turns to walk inside the store.

"Hey, fags." Craig looks directly at Ben and John.

Both of them look down and don't say anything back as they start to get back into the car. They seat up and strap in, ready to make another attempt at finding the famous graveyard.

"God, I hate this town." Ben looks out the window away from John. They sit in silence while "Burning Down the House" by Talking Heads plays on the radio.

"Watch out, you don't know who you're after," the young men yell at the top of the lungs, the music takes the boy's minds off the long trip for a minute.

A little more than an hour later, the two-thrill seekers reach their destination – or "Final Destination," as Ben keeps referring to it.

John has repetitively asked him not to call it that anymore, cause it's stupid. So every sentence Ben has spoken since that moment has somehow involved the words "Final Destination."

The car slows to a halt as they drive up to the huge gate entryway to the cemetery. "I think we are walking from here." The thrill-seekers agree.

The two decide to park the vehicle right in front of the entrance gates on a shallow pile of gravel. The two exit the car, lock it, walk to the trunk and grab the survival tools from inside the backpack. Each one has a flashlight in hand and a cold one in the other as they walk slowly up to the withered old front gate.

"I guess we just pull it open. I mean, I don't see any chains or locks anywhere," Ben says, examining his surroundings.

"Okay, you do it," John exclaims.

"Bullshit, we're both gonna do it. You grab the middle, and then we'll swing this fucker open," Ben says in charge all of the sudden.

The two teens grab the gate and pull outwards till it's open just enough for the two of them to squeeze through the entrance. Both of them, flashlight ready, beer in hand, walk slowly around inside of the gate and onto the front of the cemetery's lawn.

"It's supposed to be in the back, right?" Ben questions unsurely.

Games Without Frontiers

"Yeah, I think so," John assures, while pointing the brighter, more long-distance of the two flashlights around the outer edge of the graveyard. "Hey look." He points the flashlight over the horizon in the very back corner of the cemetery.

"I think that's it." The light reflects off a rather large object.

"Okay, I guess that's it. You can kinda see the shadow of it. Right there."

John traces his flashlight around the corners of the rather large shadow. The two adventurers head across the graveyard to oldest part, all the way in the back. As they move further and further with every little step, they notice they are now closer to the backyard and a large distance from the front entrance, where their car is safely parked.

"It's do-or-die time," Ben sighs, as they step up to the huge tomb.

The thing is at least about ten feet long and wide, about four feet up in the air. High enough so that when they go to sit on the edge, they actually have to hop up. They fearlessly hop onto the top and sit on the roof while studying the sides underneath their behinds with the flashlights, noticing that the side of the huge tomb are etched with children's names and ages: 'O Conner, seven; Straider, four; Himan, six; and Thicke, two. One name grabs Ben's attention, so he shines his flashlight directly to it. "Look at that name, ha-ha!" Ben exclaims.

"Huh." John turns and looks to where the flashlight is pointing. He starts laughing. "Ha-ha, A. Gorilla." They both roar with laughter, so loud it can be heard echoing throughout the land of the dead.

Then Ben quickly shushes them and asks, "Do you hear that?"

"Oh come on, asshole."

"No, I really think I hear something. It sounds like whimpering."

"Oh shit, I heard it too. I just didn't want to say anything."

"I think it's coming back over there, from behind us."

They both Illuminate the area in the back left corner where several pretty large headstones that must be hundred years old are.

"Listen, there it is again."

John hops off one side of the tomb, and Ben stands on top, holding the flashlight and the billy club very tightly. "Hello?"

No answer. The young men are very apprehensive at this moment and are not sure what exactly is going on. The thought crosses Ben's mind that while he is standing on top of this thing, something from beyond might come up and knock him off of it.

"Dude, I'm scared," Johns says quickly.

"Yeah, me too." He agrees with John but is not quite ready to give up.

Games Without Frontiers

Ben thought they would have a better chance of fighting something off if they were both aware, instead of being caught off guard or frightened trying to find their way back to the entrance. "Hello?" It was a much louder *hello* this time than the last.

"Maybe we should get out of here, like right now," John says cautiously, taking a few small steps back in the direction of the entrance, eyeing each step very carefully.

Then out of nowhere a very loud cry of "help" burst's out from behind one of the large gravestones in the corner.

Both flashlights go immediately to this location, and two shadows are moving around quite franticly, as if a struggle is taking progress.

Ben jumps off the tomb onto the ground and runs very quickly to where the fighting is taking place. John follows, but not as quickly. Ben runs up to the headstone, pointing the flashlight directly at it, and discovers two people are behind it. As he gets closer, he realizes that one of them is a young girl and the other is an older man well into his forties.

"No, help! No. Help me, please!"The girl is screaming at the top of her head now. The girl breaks free from the man and runs to Ben. She ducks behind him, grabbing him very firmly by the chest. She is sobbing and hysterical. John is close now too. The three of them form a small protective group.

Ben and John both hold the flashlights, blinding the older man, and as he brushes his eyes to see again, the boys notice a can of mace in his hand.

"Whoa, whoa, what the hell are you kids doing here? This is private property," the creep shouts at the three of them at the top of his lungs.

"We're ghost hunting. What's your excuse?" Ben realizes he said something kinda cool, but he has no time to think about it now. A million thoughts are going through his mind, and he can barely think at all on top of the fact the he is scared within an inch of his life, fearing the old man's excuse.

"Oh my god, please just go," the girl exclaims from Ben's chest. "Just go. What are you gonna do kill all of us?" She stares directly at the old man

"You kids – you stupid fucking kids – I should kill you."

"Look asshole," Ben says, pointing the bat at the old man.

"You may have some fucking pussy-ass pepper spray, but there are three of us, and I will knock you the fuck out with this bat if you come one motherfucking step closer."

The old man lowers his hands now, as his eyes have adjusted to the bright light being shone in his face. He begins to creep up a little bit and lowers his hands all the way down to his side like he's about to do something.

Games Without Frontiers

"Don't even think about it, old man. Look, one of us may go to the hospital tonight, but I guarantee your perverted old ass is going to the fucking morgue. Test me, bitch."

Some sense seems to have finally come to the dirty old man, he backs away from the group and then turns jogging off the other way. The three waste no time at all. Ben grabs the girl and takes off running with John doing the very same. No one stops until they've reached the car and all are safely inside.

John whips the keys out of his pocket, starts the car, turns on the headlights, floors the gas, and turns, looking over his shoulder all at the same time. In no time, they are safely out of the graveyard road and back on street, flying down the highway to safety.

"What the fuck was going on back there?" Ben exclaims at the top of his lungs, now leaning back in the seat and being able to actually take a breath.

"Thank you, thank you, oh my god," the girl says under her breath.

"What's your name?" John says, steering the wheel and directing his question to the girl. "That's Ben. I'm John."

"Alice."

"Nice to meet you, Alice."

Ben turns and extends his hand towards the backseat. She shakes his hand with a small laugh under her breath.

John holds his hand up and she shakes his as well.

"How did you manage to find your way out to Wonderland?" Ben asks with a sly tone, and John looks at Ben right in the eyes, trying not to laugh.

"What?" she asks, sounding a little confused.

"Why were you in a graveyard in the middle of the night?"

"I snuck out of my house to go see my boyfriend. To get to his house, you can cross through a few woods and the cemetery, and you're right there."

As she explains herself, the news of a boyfriend has a mild effect on both of the young men. "When I got to his house, I found he had fallen asleep, and I couldn't wake him up." She takes a brief pause, still trying to catch her breath.

Ben is turned around looking at her and is thinking about how pretty this girl looks. Through all of the circumstances, you would think she would look like shit; but no, she was a sexy little thing. All she had on was a T-shirt and pajama pants. She looked like she had all ready gotten ready to go to bed, hair up in a ponytail and no makeup on.

"So I left his house and was coming back home when a van pulled up next to me, and that asshole started trying to get me to get in. When I wouldn't, he jumped out of the car and grabbed me and tried to toss me in the back. He sprayed me in the eyes with mace, and I took off running through the cemetery."

Games Without Frontiers

"But he caught up to me. I mean I couldn't see anything."

"Hey, as long as you're okay now," John says sweetly to her.

"Yeah, this is really weird. We were actually looking for ghost when I said that back there," Ben laughs.

"Oh, I don't what I would have done without you guys. Y'all are like my heroes now," she says, smiling and finally getting a little comfortable in the car, realizing how close she actually came to being raped and maybe killed. "Wow, I can't believe that just happened."

"Yeah, it's over now," Ben reassures her while putting his hand on her knee. He didn't realize until after he had done it that he had touched her, and it was the first time a girl had ever let him put his hand her. This makes a small smile come across his face.

She notices the hand as well, and feels a small amount of comfort across her entire body, which is very nice for both of them after what they had all experienced.

"Is there somewhere you want us to take you?"

She gives John directions to her home. She has to sneak back in through the bedroom window, so everyone is being quiet. She hugs and kisses John on the cheek, gets out of the car with Ben, and walks up to her window. She turns to him and says, "Thank you." She looks him right in the eyes and moves in closer and kisses him on the lips, holds for a second, and then leans her head back. "I'll see ya."

She smiles and climbs through the window and shuts it behind her.

As Ben turns to walk away, she peeks her head out of the window one last time says, "Please promise me you won't tell anyone about this? Please?"

"It's our secret." Ben walks to the car and gets in the passenger seat.

"Wow," Ben says.

"Can we go home now?"John asks in a funny tone.

"Yes," Ben shouts in very happy way. They both laugh. "Hey dude will you do me a favor?"

"Yeah, man."

"I promised her I wouldn't tell anyone about this, so can we keep this between us?"

"Ha, are you crazy?"

"Yeah, I might be."

When the boys returned to school after the weekend, the story had already begun to circulate. Their friendship was never the same. Ben for some reason felt betrayed, but he did like his version of the story better then John's, so after some time went by he felt comfortable talking about it. When he started telling his version of the story, which was much more intimate, it became a bigger hit than John's version.

3.

Oct '00s

Paul was exhausted after his first year at college. Sure, the parties were awesome, and the classes weren't that bad. It was shuffling school, full-time work, and commuting between both, which was a forty-five minute journey each way. So spending around three hours a day driving became more than anyone could handle. Joining the Marines always seemed like a better idea to him. He was much more interested in that. He continued showing interest until he finally went a recruiter's office and enlisted. He had to drop a little weight and was still regularly exercising.

He moved in with one of his buddies, Miles, who was trying to work with full-time school as well.

The two of them met at school and worked waiting tables at the same restaurant, where they became very aware of the beverage scam, gift-card rip off, short change, wrong order (keep the right one for yourself) and everyone's favorite "The Goat." All the many splendors of the service business were at their bay. Today was gonna be Paul's big payoff before he left.

Tonight would be the last night Paul would be home for a while, because the next morning he would be on his way to Paris Island. This was going to be a night to remember.

This would be his final shift on the floor, most likely forever. So he kept some three hundred dollars in unused gift cards. This was going to be play money. Cashing out the gift cards but never taking off the totals was a great way to make some big easy money. As his final shift on the floor was nearing its end, he walked around, saying his goodbyes to everyone. He hugged Jennifer, who he would be seeing at nine; then he hugged Kaitlin, who he would be seeing around twelvish, maybe even a little later. This was gonna be a night to remember. Paul didn't give a shit if he and his friends "ripped the roof off his motherfucking apartment" that night. He knew this was gonna be interesting.

As soon as work is over, he rushes to the liquor store and buys a half gallon of vodka.

Games Without Frontiers

Paul finishes a joint pulling out of the liquor store parking lot on his way home.

As he walks into the duplex, his roomy, Miles, walks out of his room. "Is dat P-Money?"

"Wassup?" They slap their hands together firmly, like real men.

"You ready for this shit?"

"Hell yeah!"

Paul places the bottle on the counter with an offering. "Shot?"

"Don't mind if I do." They toast glasses properly, like real gentlemen. Miles is, for some reason, holding a bottle of whiskey now that has to seem to have come out of nowhere. The two men take a gargantuan swig from each other's weapon of choice. "Burr," they both make a horrible face as the golden poison runs down their throats. It's a magnificent feeling.

Miles walks over to the counter, sets his bottle down on it and then walks over to the stereo, sitting all alone in the living room. Paul had moved his things out the day before and put them in storage, so their place was pretty bare. The stereo comes on with some Bon Jovi the boys sing, "Shot in the heart, and you're to blame. You give love a bad name." They dance around the empty living room, and Paul can't help but think how small everything looks in the bare apartment.

Normally the two were very careful with the place and were very neat, but tonight neither one of them gave a shit.

Just as Paul starts pouring a shot for the two of them, there's a knock on the door. Miles walks to the door and opens it. As the door opens, Samantha, one of Paul closest girlfriends for a while, comes running in and gives him a huge hug. They offer her a shot, and she accepts.

"Buah!" she says after she swallows the drink. "Hey, Paul?"

"Yeah."

"Wanna a body shot?"

"You know I do!"

She lies on the empty counter-top of the bar and pulls up her shirt and exposes a nipple, just barely. Both gentlemen were hoping for more than just a little nipple. They would have loved to see the whole thing. Miles pours the shot in her stomach, and Paul sucks it out and cleans up any spillage with his tongue. He just so happens to lick her stomach completely clean. As he leans back, Samatha leans up and French-kisses him. The kiss ends up lasting a lot longer than it should. They do more shots till everyone's a little toasted.

Miles gets a phone call and walks away from the living room and out onto the balcony so he can hear the call.

At just that moment, some Motley Crue song starts playing on the stereo. And Paul is kissing Samatha before he knows it. So they go to the bedroom where there is nothing but a mattress on the floor. They fuck for about twenty minutes. She comes, he comes, and all is wrapped in half an hour.

Games Without Frontiers

They put their clothes on. She hugs him, and they walk to the front door together.

"I'm really gonna miss you." She looks at him and smiles, and then turns to Miles. "Bye Miles." She waves.

"Bye, babe. Good seeing ya."

She kisses Paul one more time on the lips and then heads to her car. Paul never saw her ever again. This was going to be the last time he saw a lot of people. It was going to count.

"One to me"

"Oh, that shits not fair," Miles exclaims. "She came here just for you. It's not like she just showed up not knowing anyone or anything."

"Fuck you. It counts."

It is barely four in the afternoon, still plenty early to wreck shop. Miles and Paul continue to have multiple shots. They finally stop because they don't want to get too drunk, they had people coming over and passing out was definitely not on this evening's agenda. So the drinking and smoking weed was kept to a minimum. It was not only his responsibility to be at the bus at 0400 the next morning, it was also Miles' job. As long as he was at the drop off on time, nothing else mattered really.

Hours pass in a haze, which was not intended. Everyone throughout the evening comes and goes with not much worth noting, other than their goodbyes and hugs.

Drinks continue, and at one point Paul even enjoys a line of complementary coke. Paul fights to stay awake.

Opening his eyes wide open for the first time in a while, he realizes that he is being driven in a car somewhere. Paul checks his hands to make sure that he is not handcuffed. Relief washes over his body. He looks to see who is chaffering him.

Paul looks to the driver. She is a young girl, pretty with blonde hair and green eyes; he is certain he's never seen this person before.

"Hi," Paul mutters.

"Hey," the girl responds with a quick glance and short smile.

"This may sound weird, but how did I get here?" Paul says with a little embarrassment in his tone.

"Oh don't worry, sweetie. I'm gonna get you there on time. Don't worry."

A glimpse of Paul's future plays quickly through his mind, and he begins to worry a little more. "Oh shit, I'm supposed to be going in to the Marines today."

"I know, you've told me at least ten times now."

"Oh, my bad, I'm sorry."

"Quit apologizing. Every thing's fine."

"So my names ... Paul." He begins to reach his hand out to offer a shake. The girl extends her hand to his, and they gently shake.

Games Without Frontiers

"I'm Erin."

"Hi, Erin."

"Hi, Paul." She smiles and continues to drive, unaffected by the conversation. "We'll be there in five minutes, and you'll still be almost an hour early."

"Oh, thank god," Paul exclaims. "I honestly didn't know what was going on for a second there. I don't even know where you came from."

They both laugh a little uncomfortably, and the mood in the car begins to feel at ease. Paul checks his things and then remembers that pretty soon none of those possessions are going to matter.

"So, Paul, why do you want to be a Marine?" Erin asks.

"It's something I've always thought about doing, and right now in my life it seems like the best decision."

"Well, that makes sense." Erin nods her head, seemingly agreeing with him. "You sure you didn't just want to blow shit up?"

Paul smiles to this and returns, "Life has its little bonuses." Their eyes meet mid-sentence, and it is at that exact moment Paul realizes he has fallen in love. This girl, at this moment, is the sexiest thing he had ever laid his eyes on.

The two continue chatting all the way to Paul's stop. When they get there, he slides out of the car, and with his one last moment of his civilian life, he asks Erin, "Do you think I will ever see you again?"

"Maybe."

That one word is how he survived the next three months

4.

May '00s

The city is quiet today for some reason. Ben doesn't care what the reason is; it was nice to get some sleep. It had been a long week. The day began around three in the afternoon, which didn't really matter today: off from work; no school. Ben was finishing off some school projects into the late hours and was still extremely hungover from the bottle of vodka he was finishing off as well.

Ben stands up from his bed and walks to the toilet. In the middle of urinating, he begins throwing up quite a bit. Ben lies down next to the toilet to catch his breath in between the vomiting spells. After he is finished, he gets up and walks into the bedroom. Ben sits on the edge of the bed and searches for the remote control for the television, giving up after about ten seconds. He stands up and reaches over to the TV to flip it on manually. Still standing up, he clicks through the channels until one is showing something interesting.

He stops flipping when he sees what looked like a police chase show – always interesting. He leaves the television alone and searches for hair of the dog that had bit him the previous evening.

Ben spots the bottle on the floor, and before he even knew what he was doing, the bottle was turned back and elixir is running down his throat. After the big gulp, he lets out an amazingly loud sigh of relief. "Today is gonna be nice," he thinks aloud. Ben lies on the bed, drinking and watching the television, until he hears the phone ring. After leaning up to get up off the bed, Ben relaxes and just lets the answering machine intercept the call. The voice on the machine is loud enough to hear, and if it is important, he will just call them back.

"Hey, Ben. It's Chase. Uhhhh, call me at, uhhhh … I'll just come by later."

Ben was already prepared mentally for Chase to come over, so he didn't see much purpose in the phone call other than to reconfirm that Chase would be over at Ben's apartment soon. Ben lies back onto his bed and lets out a huge sigh. "Ahhhhhhh, time to get up."

After standing up and stretching, Ben paces to the balcony of his apartment, walks outside and lights a cigarette. It's pretty cold outside, so Ben smokes quickly, careful not to waste the cigarette but making sure it's a quick one. Halfway through the cigarette, looking out over his balcony down at everyone below, Ben notices Chase's car pull up into an empty parking space in front of Ben's building.

Games Without Frontiers

"Hey man!" Ben shouts towards Chase when he gets out of his car.

Chase turns around and yells back to Ben. "Wassup."

Ben walks to the front door and unlocks it. Then walking to the living room a loud knock on the door. "Come in."

"Hey," Chase says under his breath as he swings the front door wide open and quickly steps into the apartment with his hands full of different things.

"Whatcha got there?" Ben asks, pointing to Chase's stack of things.

"I brought my laptop, the camera, and some tapes." Dropping everything on the kitchen table, Chase begins sorting through the items, shuffling them from one side of the table to another, as if to organize. Ben walks to the table and opens the laptop Chase has put there. He flips open the screen and turns the labtop on. While it's booting up, he plugs it in to the wall so the battery won't go out while the two are working.

Chase puts everything in order on the table and sits down next to Ben saying, "Yeah, you got to see some of this new stuff I got." He starts clicking folders and opening up different processes on the computer.

Ben walks into the bedroom while Chase is powering everything up and grabs the bottle of vodka. Ben walks back to the kitchen table. "Shot?"

Chase looks up ever so quickly and answers, "Yes, please."

Ben walks to the kitchen and grabs two shot glasses and fills them up.

"Cheers." The two men toast glasses and then drink up. Ben and Chase both take a big swig of orange juice from the gallon jug that Paul grabbed out of the refrigerator.

"So anyway..." Chase redirects his attention to the laptop. "So I've got the video down to ten minutes. I cut all that junk out from the middle. It was taking too long."

"Yeah, did you decide on any music yet?" Ben asks.

"Yeah, since it doesn't matter if it's copyrighted or not, I've got Moby and Chemical Brothers songs I think I'm gonna use during the transitions."

Ben and Chase are partners on an editing project for their editing class. They were already nearly finished and just polishing off some minor details, such as sound and music. The two enrolled in the film class for very different reasons. Paul needed the credit, so it wasn't anything more than an easy blow-off class. Chase was quite the opposite. He believed himself to be the reincarnation of Hitchcock and felt destined to be the next Spielberg.

After meeting one another in class, Ben became very inspired by Chase and his passion for film. Ben had never really understood all the things it takes to make a movie, but now his eyes were wide open.

Games Without Frontiers

The grueling unforgiving setting of any film intrigued Ben very much. Something woke up inside Ben during those days; he realized that his calling was one for the movies. The two students had become pretty close friends throughout the semester, always working with one another on projects. If any paying jobs came up, they were sure to let each other know and were now carpooling to work on small low-budget films, commercials, and television shows.

It was the end of the semester now, and finishing the final project was the only thing the two were currently working on. It was a short film, only about eight minutes long. They shot it together and were now editing it together. Chase was already putting the finishing touches on it without consulting with Ben, who didn't really mind much. The film was a silly little comedy about a friend and his roommate getting into an argument and then resolving their troubles in an unorthodox way.

It only took an afternoon to film with Chase behind the camera and Ben playing one of the roommates. They had everything they needed for the short film; now they were just putting all the pieces together in editing.

"So what do you want to name this thing?" Ben asks.

"Not sure. Any ideas?"

"I was thinking maybe 'the Cowboys.'"

"Really? Why's that?"

"'Cause I'm wearing a Dallas Cowboys jersey, and that's how the whole argument starts."

"True. Yeah, that would work."

"Dude, if you've got anything better, let me know."

"No, I like it. I mean, we've got to think of something kinda quick." Chase pulls up the title of the projects and types in 'The Cowboys.' "Done."

The two continue working for a while until someone knocks on the front door. Ben stands and walks to the door, calling out, "Who is it?"

A voice can be heard shouting through the door: "Keith."

"Just a sec." Ben opens the door. "What's going on?"

"Oh, not a lot. Just seeing what you're up to." Keith walks in the front door.

"Keith, this is Chase. Chase, this is Keith, my downstairs neighbor."

"Hey," they say at the same time. Keith is significantly older than the two twenty year olds, by about fifteen years. Keith and Ben hang out regularly. They had met one day outside the apartment while smoking cigarettes.

Keith always seemed to have something interesting going on, and it broke the monotony of Ben's usual nothing-to-do.

Keith sits down on the couch with his attention on the television. "What are you watching?"

"Oh, nothing. We were working on this class project, editing a little movie together," Ben answers.

"Cool. What's your movie about?"

"The Cowboys," Chase says with a smile on his face.

"Yeah, it kinda is," Ben directs to Keith. "But it's more than that."

"Of course it is, but you got to keep the title quick, right. I mean, I don't know; you're the movie guru." Then Keith casually says, "Hey, Ben?"

"Yeah, Keith."

"Can I bum a smoke?"

"I'll join you," Ben says, standing up and walking to the balcony. Keith also stands and joins him. They walk outside while Chase still sits working on the project.

Outside Keith leans against the railing, and Ben pulls out two cigarettes from his pack, handing one to Keith. He lights Keith's cigarette first and then his own. "So what's going on, Keith?"

"Awww, nothing. I kinda wanted to see if you would be interested in something."

"It depends on what that something is," Ben says between drags of his smoke.

"I've got this little bit of ice that I need to get rid of. Interested?"

"Can I see it?"

"Sure." Keith reaches into his pocket and pulls out a tiny little Ziploc bag out. He hands it to Ben.

Ben examines the small little bag. it is only about a fifth full, but still enough. "How much?"

"Twenty."

"Sold." Ben walks inside with the bag, puts it on the counter and picks up his billfold. Ben shuffles through some dollar bills, grabs a twenty, puts the wallet down, and walks back to the balcony to hand Keith the money.

"Thank you, sir." Keith grabs the bill from Ben and puts it into his pocket. "All right, well I'm gonna head. Got some stuff to take care of."

"All right, man." Ben pats Keith on the back and walks him to the front door to let him out. "Later."

"Later, buddy." Keith puts his hand up, waving to Ben and Chase as he exits the apartment.

"What was all that about?" Chase asks.

"I just bought some speed," Ben answers non chalantly, picking up the little Ziploc bag and bringing it to the table for them both to examine.

"No shit."

"No shit. You want some?" Ben pours a small amount of the white powder onto the table and then uses a credit card to make lines.

Games Without Frontiers

Ben stands up, walks to the kitchen, and finds a plastic straw, which he cuts into a two inch version of its former self.

"Yeah, I guess," Chase says with not much confidence in his voice.

"It will make me stay up for a while, won't it?"

"Yeah, you'll probably be up for the next day and half, and you probably won't eat anything."

"Why won't I eat anything?"

"Because this shit makes you not hungry."

"Oh."

"Still want some?"

"Sure." Chase looks halfway determined now, ready for anything. Ben sits at the table with the straw, puts the straw to his nose and snorts a line. After that, he hands Chase the straw, and Chase snorts a line for himself. They alternate, until all of the white powder is gone. "Holy shit. We're in for a ride, aren't we?"

"Oh yeah." This was Chase's first time obviously, and Ben wants to make sure he doesn't freak him out. "Don't worry man. It's fun. The comedown's a bitch though."

"What do you mean?"

"When this stuff wears off, your gonna get really depressed. I suggest you drink some alcohol, so you will be able to try and get some sleep when that happens."

"Okay."

It takes about fifteen minutes till they both really feel the drug starting to kick in.

Just in time for them to finish the last touches on their project. "And done." Chase clicks on his laptop and closes the files.

Ben finds a copy of *The Matrix* and puts it into the DVD player. They migrate to the living room and get comfortable to watch the movie. They're only thirty minutes in when Ben opens the windows and proclaims that they don't have to go outside to smoke anymore. They make an ash tray out of a glass with some water in the bottom, and before they know it they're out of cigarettes. They decide to go the store and get some things.

Ben starts realizing how messed up he is beginning to feel on the way to the convenient store. With the passenger window rolled all the way down, Ben can feel the cold air against his face, and it feels really good. Chase parks his car in the front of an EZ mart, and Ben gets out of the car. Before walking inside, he asks Chase if they need anything besides cigarettes. Chase can't think of anything, so Ben walks to the front and buys four packs of smokes.

On the way back to Ben's apartment, Chase starts up a conversation about the new *Star Wars*. "I was watching the extras. It showed how they storyboarded and filmed the fight scene inside the volcano."

"Really? I need to check that out."

"Yeah, I'll let you borrow it."

Games Without Frontiers

"Cool." Ben is already smoking and still enjoying the fresh air. "You know, Chase, I really have become interested in this whole movie thing."

"Yeah, I've loved this stuff my entire life."

"It's weird, but now I feel as though it's my calling." Ben smiles. "You know, it's just something that I really want to do with my life now."

"I know, man. It's exciting stuff, isn't it?"

Chase pulls up to the apartment, and the two walk back into Ben's place.

Both men are feeling pretty good. They debate for a few minutes, now that *The Matrix* is going off, on what they should watch next.

"How about *Gladiator*?" Ben asks Chase.

"How about *Heat*?" Chase looks at Ben's DVD's on the shelves. Ben grabs the DVD of *Heat* and puts it in the DVD player. The film begins playing on the television, and Ben sits back down on the couch and lights up another cigarette. Neither of them pays much attention to the film but continue to have what seems like long, well thought-out conversations. Things like, "What happens when you die?" or "Do you think aliens are real?" The drugs made the two of them very talkative. "See, this why *Heat* is such a great movie. It has all three things to make a great ending to great movie." The film's final scene plays. Both guys sit quiet.

Out of curiosity, Ben asks, "What are the three things that make a great ending?"

"All great works of fiction have a death, a confrontation, and then a thought that is usually the meaning. In *Heat*, it's Pacino playing Hanna and De Niro playing McCauley, only the two of them, both willing to kill one another, so they are head to head in a confrontation. Then Hanna gets the drop on McCauley and kills him – that's the death – and then they hold hands, because Hanna tries to comfort him and McCauley looks up and tells him he's never going back, so these last things they say to one another was the meaning."

"Interesting theory," Ben notes.

"All the great ones have it, if you think about it." Chase seems proud of himself.

After a while with the drugs kicking in a little more, Ben starts telling Chase about a recurring dream he keeps having. "There's, like, this builder in the dream. He's, like, building a glass house, and I go up to him and ask if he needs help, and he tells me yes. So I'm putting glass walls up on the foundation."

"Who's the guy building the house?" Chase asks.

"I don't know, but we know each other somehow," Ben continues. "It's strange, because we keep building the glass house up and we roof it and basically finish it off completely. And we're sitting there looking at the house, the man and me, and he decides to get up and walk into the house."

Games Without Frontiers

"And I shout out that it's not a real house, and all of the sudden it shatters into glass."

"Wow."

"Yeah, and the next thing I know, I'm running up to the house as it collapses on this guy, trying to help him. But it's too late by then. He just dies there." Ben goes quiet when he says this and repeats. "He just lays there and dies. No matter how much I try and help him."

"How often do you have this dream?" Chase quietly interrupts.

"Like, every few months or so, I guess," Ben re-affirms himself.

"You think it means something?"

"I don't know."

5.

August '00s

For the months after Paul graduated the academy, he made a few visits back home. During the first visit, Paul made sure he found Erin and asked her out on a date. The two were looking forward to each of the visits. By then, they were officially seeing each other.

Today Paul was in Japan. During the afternoon that day, he called Erin back in the US, but there was no answer. Paul was looking forward to the weekend. His plans were completely open. He started the evening with a few of his Jarhead buddies. Beers and shots all around.

The guys always had money to burn on the weekends, so it was a spectacle of some sorts when the guys got together. After a few hours of drinking and singing karaoke at the Golden Dragon, Paul and his buddy "Jeffries" made their way down the street.

"Hey, Jeffries."

"Yeah."

"Where's that place where they light the drinks on fire?"

"Ugh, Ku-Ma-Za's, I think."

"Yeah. Yeah, I think that's it. Let's go there."

"Cool."

The two men walk down the foreign streets, sticking out like a sore thumb. "I love Japan," Paul hollers out at the top of his lungs. "Whew!"

"Ha-ha." They both laugh.

"Paul, if we get there and it's packed, we can go back to the East side. There's bound to be something going on over there."

"Sure. I'm thinking about getting a hooker. I need to get laid." Paul sounds very serious. "We need to go get some pussy."

"Fuck, ya. Shit, let's go back to that place around the other side of town."

Paul knew exactly which whorehouse Jeffries was talking about. They had frequented it several times. "I agree." Paul nods. "Let's get a few drinks first."

The two men agree on this and begin heading towards a small sake place simply called Chow that also serves hard liquor. On the way to Chow, instead of catching a ride to the bar, they continue walking until they're at a street corner, waiting for the red light to change.

Paul looks at Jeffries and says, "Me gonna get some sucky sucky."

"Hell yeah," agrees Jeffries.

"I've been waiting for this shit all week," Paul exclaims on the street corner. "Hey, what's the name of those drinks, you know the ones where they light 'em up?"

"Man, I can't remember, but everyone gets one so all you'll have to do is point."

"True."

Paul, standing on the corner, began to realize that he had learned basically no Japanese during his entire time spent in the country. Paul laughs a little, just enough for Jeffries to hear.

"What are you laughing about?" Jeffries asks.

"Oh nothing, just the fact I've been here over a month, and I haven't learned any Chinese." Paul says with a small amount of humor in his tone.

"You do know they speak Japanese here, in Japan," Jeffries assures Paul.

"Oh yeah," Paul bust out. "I can't tell one fucking slanty-eyed dink from another."

Noticing that there are people around them who they might have offended, Paul and Jeffries haul ass across the small street, and as they reach the corner Chow has become slightly more visible. The place is not real crowded but seems busy.

Games Without Frontiers

"There it is," they agree.

Walking casually into the bar, they notice that there's a small party of US marines at one table already. It's Parker, Jones, and Enrickson, some of the other guys stationed with them on the base. They wave at Paul and Jeffries to come over and join them, which they do.

They order five flaming Ryu's and pound the drinks as soon as they arrive. Enrickson, a young, small white guy, can barely hold his liquor; and after this round, it will be his fourth. Enrickson's declares to the entire bar that "America is the best country on earth" and that he misses his country. Jones and Jeffries start refraining him to speak while chuckling through the whole ordeal.

A small group of people are singing "Don't Stop Believing" on the karaoke machine in the back of the bar turn and notices the yelling.

"Hey, Parker, why don't you get the private out of here before he makes a mess of things," Paul says, looking straight at Parker with a condescending look. Parker is a young good looking african american, who seems to always be in high spirits, even though Paul always gives him a hard time.

"Yeah, I can get him out of here, no problem." Parker makes the best of being asked to leave with Enrickson, trying not to let the fact that Paul had basically ordered him to do it bother him.

Paul was always on Parker's ass about little things he did before Paul was made sergeant, and now that Paul was Parker's officer, Parker had no questions and just simply had to follow orders. Parker had a small theory about Paul being a racist, because he always specifically singled Parker out every time he did anything remotely wrong. Not only would he single him out, but Paul would make an entire situation look like Parker's fault when he didn't have anything to do with it to begin with.

"You can do that no problem – *what*?" Paul etches his head closer to Parker with sheer magnificence in his eyes.

"I can do that no problem, sir," Parker says with a very stern face.

Parker picks up Enrickson and walks him sturdily to the front door, pushes it open and leaves.

"Hey, Jones, you want to come with me and Jeffries to the cat house," Paul offers to Private Jones.

"Sure enough. No wait a minute. Fuck, no, I better not." Jones reluctantly shrugs his shoulders and continues.

"No, man, I got this girl I like back stateside, and if I get anything I can't shake off, she won't have nothing to do with my ass."

"All right, Pussy." Paul smiles at Jones, very snarky. "We will tell you all about it back at HQ, ha-ha."

"All right then. All right."

Games Without Frontiers

Paul wants Jones to say, "All right then, *sir*," but even though he doesn't, it really doesn't bother Paul very much. At this point, all three men are pretty intoxicated, and Paul decides to leave without Jeffries, who no longer wants to get any and just wants to go back to base.

Paul leaves the bar and walks down some back alleyways, certain that he has found a shortcut. The alleyways are narrow and dark, seemingly empty. Nothing much around is illuminated except for a few street lights every now and then. Paul begins feeling a bit nervous in the back alleys as he walks alone. A feeling of drunkenness and fright are consuming him in what is now feeling like a never-ending set of alleys. Paul picks up the pace to a steady fast walk. The hairs on his neck are standing up for some reason. Finally, making way down this endless path, he hears, "Hey, American. You want to see something?"

Quickly Paul turns around and realizes he's not alone in the back alley. In the shadows, there is a small Japanese man. Paul wants to run, but when he looks down the path, he can see another Asian guy walking up towards him with a baseball bat in hand. When Paul looks back at the one who yelled at him, he is much closer and lurking towards Paul.

"Oh shit," Paul mutters to himself, knowing that these men were most likely about to attack him.

"What do you fuckers, want?" Paul yells out, keeping his stance in case one of them tries something.

"The money, motherfuck." The man is now very close to Paul, and he can see the man is carrying a knife in front of him. The two men are surrounding him with weapons, and Paul is going to be ready if they decide to attack. Paul takes the money out of his pocket. He has all of the bills held together with a money clip. Paul tosses the wad of cash to the man with the knife.

"I don't want any trouble." Paul's still trying to reason. "I gave you the money. Now let me go." The guy with the knife picks up the money and puts it in his pocket, and then with the slightest gesture he nods to his friend behind Paul.

Paul ducks when the mugger behind him swings the bat directly at his head – and misses. Paul charges into the thug and knocks the bat out of his hands, and then head-butts the attacker with a sudden hard thrust, which knocks the man out cold. The other Asian man starts to take off running with Paul's money, but before he can get far, Paul picks up the recently freed baseball bat and throws it at the thug with all his might. The bat hits the man in the upper back and lower neck, which makes him fall to the ground.

Paul, feeling very proud of himself for taking out the two men, walks toward the one with his money. The man is lying, sobbing in pain, on the ground. Step by causal step, Paul makes his way over and picks up the baseball bat from the street.

Games Without Frontiers

He takes a few practice swings. "You fucking yellow bastards like baseball, right?" Paul asks during the swings. The man still lies on the on the ground, sobbing.

His buddy, also lying on the ground, isn't making any noise because he is completely unconscious.

The thug that Paul is taunting tries to crawl away.

"I love baseball. You want to see the American hit one out of the park?" Paul is now only a step away from the thug lying there in enormous pain. Paul picks up his money from the guy's pocket and puts back in his possession. "I'm gonna knock one right out of the park just for you, my fellow yellow."

Now standing directly in front of the thief, Paul raises the bat up over his head and comes down with the bat as hard as he can. The man's head splits open a bit, and blood is gushing all over the alley now. "That's how I roll, motherfucker." Paul spits on the man, drops the bat, and continues on the path he originally intended, which eventually leads out to a street he recognizes. His blood is boiling still from the fight and he feels extremely good about the fate he just dealt to the two thieves. However, he no longer feels like going to get a prostitute, even though he has enough money to get like three or four of them. But no, he decides to keep his twenty dollars for something else and makes his way back to the base.

Paul enters his section and goes to his room. He undresses and lies on the bed.

Paul lets out an enormous yawn as he gets comfortable. He leans over to a small desk next to the bed, opens the door and pulls out a calling card. Paul walks out the pay phone in the hallway and dials the number on the card. When asked to put the desired number in, he dials Erin's home phone.

It rings twice, and then he hears Erin pick up. "Hello," she says, half asleep.

"Hey, it's me. You sleeping?"

"No, no, no." Erin sounds more awake now. "Hey."

"If you're sleeping, I can call back."

"No, no. I'm awake. I want to talk to you."

"How was your day?"

"Good, I got to see Charlotte and the kids."

"Oh, really? How where they?"

"Good. They asked about you."

"Did they? That's nice."

"Yeah ..."

"Yeah, what?"

"I miss you."

"I miss you, too."

"Anything happen to you today?"

"Nah."

6.

January '00s

Ben is up early today. He has a five a.m. crew time to meet,
but being more of a night person makes this especially hard for him.
The alarm is ringing, and it's the only thing you can hear throughout
the apartment. Ben turns off the alarm and looks at the time. It's
exactly four thirty in the morning. Yawning and stretching, Ben
makes his way out of the bedroom and into the kitchen. He grabs his
backpack and double checks it for all the things that might be
needed that day. There are some pens, his universal tool, a flashlight,
a spiral notebook, a clipboard, batteries and a few other items that he
might need throughout the day.

There are some clothes laid out on his drier, clean and ready to
go. Ben slips on the shorts, T-shirt and tennis shoes. Then, with
another long stretch and yawn, he says, "And here we go."

Ben picks up the keys to his car and is out the door with all his
things. It's still dark outside; no sunlight yet. Ben hops into his truck
and heads out to the shooting location.

The roads are empty. A car passes here and there, but there are no signs of life. Its quiet, and Ben is enjoying the silence while still waking up.

He intentionally keeps his car radio on a low volume. Driving his car was seamless. It gave him time to think about the fact that this was his third official job working on a set, which was very exciting, even if he was waking up this early in the morning for it. Everything about behind-the-camera work was exhilarating to Ben. He loved the attention to detail, the hectic pace, the crazy people he worked with; all of which had very strange and distinct personalities. Anytime something was on television that had his name on it, a feeling of excitement, better than sex, seized his body.

It was a truly wonderful feeling, and Ben felt very fulfilled doing these projects, even if they were small scale and the pay wasn't much. It was nice to be doing something that he was proud of.

The morning hours still haven't completely kicked in, and Ben is having a hard time trying to wake up. He pulls up to the location: an old warehouse building that is now used specifically for low-budget music videos. Today, Ben would be working on the Cesar Bling rap video. This was the first music video he had ever worked on, and he was a little nervous and a little excited.

Ben parks his car in front of the old warehouse.

Games Without Frontiers

The parking lot around it is almost full, but he still manages to get a not-too-bad spot in the middle of the lot. There are other people finding spaces and parading inside like a pack of zombies. Ben doesn't feel so bad that he is still only half asleep since everyone else is too. Ben gets out of his car, tosses his backpack around his shoulder, and then makes his way inside.

Stepping inside, the room is full of all kinds of people–everyone getting ready with their specific job. Only the crew were in the building right now. Cast call wouldn't be till ten. Cast call times are always after crew, allowing time for everything to be set up and ready so the actors can show up and do their thing. A few "hi's" are exchanged while everything is being set up. From across the room, Ben hears a voice call out, "Hey Ben, over here."

As Ben turns to look, he sees his buddy, Chase, on the other side of the room. Ben nods to Chase and walks over to join him.

"What's going on man?" Ben asks.

"Oh, nothing. I'm gonna be lifting this big ass light up on this C-stand right here." The light that Chase is referring to will be part of the key lighting for the music video. "Where are you today?"

"P.A.," Ben answers. This means he is considered a production assistant, which pretty much means that he does a lot of running around throughout the day, getting all the things that are needed such as food, coffee, bricks (camera batteries), tape, etc.

Mostly the busy work that no one else has time to do because of time constraints. Every shoot that Ben worked on was always a war-zone with people running around like crazy and doing all kinds of jobs to culminate into a finished product. It was very important for everything to look good, because the measure of success on this video was a good indication of how much work you would be able to do with the rapper. So more or less the video was extremely important for everyone to get right. "Yeah, I'll be running around and doing whatever today."

"I'm on this baby all day today." Chase points at the huge light.

"I got to lift this thing on this little crank on the side of the stand." The C-stand was awfully small looking considering the light that was being mounted on it was nearly two hundred and fifty pounds.

"Wow, you got to crank that thing up and down all day?" Ben smiles.

"Yeah, but at least I don't have to run around all day," Chase snickers.

"I know, I know." Ben looks around to see if anyone is looking and then whispers to Chase."Did you bring some, bud?"

"Naw, man. I left it. Sorry."

"It's all good. Just wondering. Well, I got to get to work." Ben pats Chase on the back and walks away.

Games Without Frontiers

Around that time, the Unit Production Manager Penny notices Ben and walks up to him.

"Hey, Ben."

"Hey, Penny."

"I've got some batteries. Can you hold on to them for me?"

"Yeah, I'll put them in my backpack." Penny hands Ben a couple of small six-volt batteries. He sticks the batteries into a pocket on his backpack. "Where do you want me today?"

"Umm." Penny looks down at her clipboard. "I'm gonna have you keeping an eye on the dancers when they get here."

"Cool."

"Until then, can you help Rob get some things off of the truck?"

"Sure." Even though he wanted to say, "No, that's not my job," like some of the other members of the crew would do.

But Ben was always willing to do anything without a fuss. It sucked, but he hoped in the end it would help get him noticed. So Ben puts down his backpack and walks outside to the equipment truck. It's parked right outside of the entrance, and the back is already open with the steps pulled out leading up into the back of the truck. Ben can hear shuffling around inside. "Rob?"

"Yeah," Rob answers from deep inside the truck.

"Hey, it's Ben. You need a hand with anything?"

"Sure, hop on up here," Rob calls out from inside the truck.

"Can you help me put all these crates on that dolly over there?"

Ben looks behind and sees the dolly that Rob is referring to. He grabs it and pushes it up to the back of the truck. Rob appears out of the darkness and starts handing Ben some small crates one by one. Ben stacks the crates neatly while Rob is handing each one to him.

"Yeah, stack it up. Leave some room on the front, because I'm gonna put some camera cases there."

"Okay," responds Ben, reasserting the items in careful order on the back-side of the crate. The two men continue till the crate is full. "I'll go ahead and roll this in there."

"'Kay." Rob turns around and disappears once again into the truck. Ben rolls the dolly cart to the front door, walks to the door and opens it, and uses a rock on the ground for a doorstop. He pulls the dolly crate inside and over to the other side of the large studio. Ben asks some of the sound guys where they want him to unload the equipment.

After they show Ben the spot where they wanted the stuff, he quietly pushes the crate over to the corner and unloads everything. Under no time constraint for this small project, Ben takes his time to casually finish the task, and then rolls the cart back outside to Rob.

As Ben rolls the cart once again up to the back of the truck, Rob pops his head out and tells Ben that Penny is looking for him.

Games Without Frontiers

"Later, Rob." Ben leaves the cart and walks inside into the inventory room where Penny usually hangs out. And sure enough, she is there, sitting at a desk. "You need me to do something for ya?"

"Yeah, the dancers will be here in a minute. Will you please see if they need anything when they get here?" Penny doesn't even turn around. She is busy sorting through some paperwork. She finally looks up and says," You'll need a headset too." She turns around from the desk and reaches for a headset. Penny grabs the walkie talkie and hands it Rob. "You're on channel two, 'kay?"

"Sure thing," Ben answers and walks over near where a small tent is set up for the dancers to change inside. No one is there yet. The girls aren't going to be there for another half hour or so, and it's still early. So Ben, making the best of his time, goes and finds a coffee kettle, fills it up with coffee and grabs some Styrofoam cups. He finds a small table next to the tent and sets the hot coffee and cups on top of it. Ben then takes a moment to clip the headset on. He turns it down till the dial is on the number two and presses on the call button. "Penny, you there?"

"What's up?" Penny responds through the headset.

"I am going to walk across the street to the store to get some milk and sugar for the girl's coffee."

"Okay, hurry back, and get a receipt."

"Sure thing." Ben still has the headset on. He leaves the building and walks across the street to a grocery store.

Ben picks up some milk and sugar, pays for it, and then heads back to the studio. Everything is still being set up and none of the dancers are there yet, still.

Ben sees a folder lying on the desk that wasn't there before with his name on it. He picks up the folder and sees it has the schedule for the day printed on the front page. He is studying the times and what was being filmed, when all of the sudden there is a loud crash, then a scream roars across the entire set. Ben recognizes the voice: it's Chase's.

Ben turns and looks to see what happened. Chase is crouching by a huge C-stand with one hand holding the other. Another crew member, a young girl, is standing next him, covering her mouth in sure dread.

Ben runs to Chase, and so does a few other crew members. "What happened," Ben yells as he gets closer.

No one answers.

Ben comes up behind his friend Chase who is shaking in dread and covered in blood. The girl standing next him is sobbing with screams. She points to the ground and says something that Ben doesn't understand at all. "Right there. It's right there," she calls out again and points to a bloody severed thumb lying alone on the floor in a small pool of blood.

"Oh my god."

Games Without Frontiers

Ben can't believe his eyes as he realizes that the thumb is missing from Chase's hand. Chase isn't saying anything, just breathing very hard. Blood is gushing from his hand. It's escaping all over the place underneath a towel Chase is holding over his hand. Penny is now standing next to Chase, trying to help him cover his wound with the towel, and Ben yells to them, "What can I do to help?"

Penny turns to Ben, still trying to help Chase, who looks like he is going to shock, and says, "Pick up his thumb and go and put it into one of the coolers in the break room. We're gonna have to take him to the hospital."

"I'll take him." Ben offers, kneeling down and picking up the severed finger. Holding the finger, Ben runs to a small cooler full of ice and sticks the thumb inside. Holding the cooler in his right hand, Ben slips off his headset with his left and sits it down on a table. Running back to Chase, he says, "I've got the finger in the cooler. I'll go pull up my car. Can you get him there, Penny?"

"Yes, hurry, Ben," Penny says under her breath, still trying to help Chase who seems to be in total shock now.

Ben doesn't waste any time. He runs full speed with the cooler to his car, jabs the keys in the ignition and starts the car. Then, hitting the gas, he flies up to the front door of the warehouse where Penny and Chase are standing. Ben pulls up to them and jumps out of his car, runs to the passenger side and lets Chase into the car.

"I've got him," Ben says and closes the door behind Chase, who is sitting, clenching his right hand and looking like he is in some sort of a daze.

"Hurry, Ben, take him to the emergency room. I'll get someone to meet you there as soon as I can, okay?"

"Yes, ma'am," Ben hollers out to her, running back to the driver seat. Ben hops into the driver seat and hits the gas pedal as hard as he can. The car screeches out of the parking lot, and Ben doesn't stop for anything. While driving anywhere between eighty to a hundred miles down the road, Ben looks at Chase and says, "It's going to be okay."

"I can't believe this shit," Chase says, staring out of the front window and seemingly not paying attention to his hand.

Ben is speeding down the road as fast as he possibly can. There is a little traffic but not much, when all of the sudden he sees police lights in his rearview mirror.

"Shit. We're getting pulled over. Don't worry, he'll probably help us," Ben assures Chase, hoping that he is right. Ben pulls the car to the side of the road, and the police car pulls up behind him. The officer walks up to the window, which Ben has already rolled down.

"Son, you in some kind of race this morning?" the cop asks Ben.

Games Without Frontiers

"Sir, my friend's been in an accident, and I'm rushing him to the hospital. His finger got cut off." Ben points to Chase's hand, and Chase holds his hand up, bloody rag and all.

The cop yells, "Holy shit … listen: I want you to follow behind me as close as you can. I'm gonna get you to the hospital, and I will call it in on our way there." The cop runs back to his car and starts down the road, flying. It takes everything inside of Ben to keep up.

The police car and Ben's car are flying through traffic with no stops at all.

Chase looks over to Ben and chuckles. "This is really cool. Well, aside from … you know." Chase holds his hand up a little.

"Don't worry, buddy; we're almost there. It's going to be all right, I promise." Ben is trying to keep Chase's mind off of how bad the situation really is. "You're gonna be fine, Chase, I promise."

Chase almost laughs when he exclaims, "I can't believe this shit. You wanna know what happened?"

"Sure. What happened?"

"I was cranking up the light with the little pulley crank on the side of the C-stand. As it was moving upward in the air, I heard something snap, and all the sudden the light was flying down on top of me, with my hand still on the crank. When the stand fell into itself, the metal bar came down on my thumb, and it just snapped it off. It flew across the room. I didn't even feel anything until that girl started screaming."

"Wow ... shit." Ben is following the cop at a high speed as they pull up to the Memorial Hospital. The cars pull into the emergency-room lane and Ben stops the car, runs out to the passenger door and opens it for Chase.

Chase gets out of the car and walks to a nurse who is running out to the car with the police officer, and he is telling her what happened to Chase's hand. "Here they are buddy. They're here."

Ben turns Chase over to the nurse, and they rush Chase inside. Ben gets back into his car and parks it in general parking, and then he realizes that Chase's finger is still in the back seat in the cooler.

He grabs the cooler and runs inside. "Here's his thumb. I've got it on ice."

A nurse comes up to Ben and takes the cooler from him. "Thank you," the nurse says." You can sit here and wait if you want."

"Okay." Ben sits down in a chair, hoping that Chase is going to be okay.

The thumb was sewed back on, even though Chase would never recover all the feeling back. It was the last time Ben would ever work together with Chase on a set ever again.

7.

April 00's

It's mid-afternoon and Paul is at the international airport, about to catch a flight back to report. This week that he was home was exceptionally awesome. Paul got to see a lot of his old friends, which was nice, but mostly he got to see Erin. They spent the entire week together and could barely keep their hands off of each other. At the end of the week, Paul proposed to Erin, and she accepted.

They plan to get married when Paul returns from Afghanistan, where he will be for the next year or so. A lot of the other guys in Paul's unit were dreading the fact that they would be in the desert for the next year, but Paul didn't really mind as he saw it as an adventure that he would never have an opportunity to do again.

The airport is pretty full, and Paul sits in military uniform at the terminal, patiently waiting for his flight. People all going in different directions. Paul ignores all the airline traffic and reads a *Entertainment Weekly* quietly.

Paul was very excited about his future as played out imaginary pictures in his head: a nice house with Erin, maybe a couple of kids running around. A small grin comes across his face while he is in deep thought.

Paul is brought back down to earth when he feels something poking at his leg, so he looks to see what it is, and there stands a little boy, probably about five years or six. The little boy stands in awe of Paul with gleaming eyes of admiration, staring straight at him.

"Do you need something, little buddy?" Paul asks in a small sweet voice.

The little boy looks up at Paul and asks, "Are you one of the good guys?"

Paul smiles and answers, "Yes, I'm one of the good guys."

"Are you gonna stop the bad guys?" The little boy looks at Paul, fully serious.

"Yep," Paul says. "That's what I'm gonna do. My name's Paul. What's yours?"

The little boy holds up five fingers and says, "I'm this many."

"Oh, so your five years old. That's cool." Paul really doesn't want to ask the kids name again, fearing that people will think it weird that a grown man is taking this much interest in a little child."Yep, I'm one of the good guys, and I'm gonna stop the bad guys."

Games Without Frontiers

Paul continues to smile at the little boy, and the boy giggles a little and looks down at the ground.

After looking at the ground for a moment, the boy looks up and half-way salutes Paul.

Paul laughs and salutes back to the kid.

"There you are! Stop bothering this man, honey." A young pale-white female, probably in her thirties, swiftly walks over and put her hands on the little boy. "Stop bothering this nice man."

Paul looks at the woman.

"It's okay, ma'am. He's not bothering me. We were just saluting each other." Paul smiles at the lady, who doesn't make eye contact with Paul. She grabs her son and holds his hand.

"I'm sorry," the lady says under her breath as she leads the little boy off in the other direction.

"Oh, it's okay. I think he'll make a mighty fine soldier one day," Paul exclaims to the woman.

"Yeah, I don't think so." Still not making any eye contact, she walks off.

"Bitch," Paul mutters quietly so no one can hear him and then returns to his magazine. After a few minutes, Paul looks to see the time. There's still about twenty minutes before they're going to start boarding for his flight. While looking up, Paul notices Parker, one of the guys in his squad, wandering around searching for an empty seat.

While looking around, Parker sees Paul, smiles and makes a small hand gesture. Parker walks over to Paul and sits down across from him.

"Hey man," Parker says in a very friendly tone. "How was your week?"

"Good." Paul looks at his magazine and doesn't bother to look up and acknowledge Parker. The two sit for a minute in uncomfortable silence.

"I can't believe it's already over. Got to see the folks, my baby mama, and my kid. Man, the little man has gotten big," Parker says, still trying to make conversation. Paul continues to ignore him. They sit in silence once again.

Out of nowhere, Parker looks directly at Paul and asks," You don't like me very much, do you?"

Paul finally looks up after the question and says," What do you mean?"

"It just seems like every one in the unit gets along, except for me and you." Parker pauses for a moment, and then starts speaking again." I mean, look, if you got a problem with me because I'm black, that's fine. I can live with that. But what I can't live with is some overbearing fucking sergeant on my ass about everything all the time."

"Look, Parker, just because you're a fuck-up doesn't mean I have anything against the color of your skin."

Games Without Frontiers

Paul laughs condescendingly towards Parker. "Look, you fucking dumb ass, you're you, and I'm me, and that's the way it is. Nothing more, nothing less."

The animosity only grew more and more between the two men in the days that followed.

8.

Sept 00's

Ben was home all day long. He skipped work, knowing that he would be fired from his job. It didn't matter. It was only a part-time deal. Earlier in the day, a girl he had been seeing over the last few weeks named Carla ended their relationship. Ben really liked the girl and was pretty upset about the entire ordeal and was drinking heavily. He was in a daze, barely still standing and walking around his apartment. The television in the living room is on and one of the Star Wars movies is playing. He wasn't really paying attention enough to even tell which one it was.

The telephone rings. Ben decides not to answer it. When he can hear his voice on the answering machine, Ben listens more carefully to see who is calling.

"Hey, Ben. Dude, I heard about Carla. Give me a call. Oh yeah, it's Chase. Call me man," Chase's voice echoes, followed by a beep. Ben stands and walks to a bottle of half-empty tequila. He unscrews the top and takes a large swig out of the bottle.

Games Without Frontiers

"Whew." Ben covers his mouth with a bit of disgust.

He stumbles to the phone and picks it up. Before he dials anything, Ben pounds the cordless phone to his head a couple of times. "Shit," Ben mutters aloud and then dials Chase's number. Hesitating for a moment because he wasn't really sure what Chase knew and wondering how he could possibly know about the breakup, Ben sits down, dialing Chase's phone number. The phone rings a couple of times.

"Hello."

"Hey, Chase, it's me man. What did you hear?"

"Oh dude, you okay? Why don't I stop by and we'll talk about it?" Chase is genuine in his voice.

"Yeah, that would be great. Come over." Ben is semi-sure that he is making the right decision extending the invite. "Later then." Ben hangs up the phone and decides to make a drink. He grabs the tequila and walks to see what's in the refrigerator to mix it with. There is a liter of Dr. Pepper that Carla most likely left there, so he picks it up and pours into an empty glass, filling it almost to the rim. Ben takes a big drink out of the tequila bottle and then swigs the Dr. Pepper. "Whew," Ben mutters under his breath and then sits the glass down and walks to his balcony. On the balcony, Ben lights a cigarette and sits on a fold-up chair, thinking very deeply.

"What am I going to do?" Ben wonders to himself. He decides that he really hasn't accomplished anything in life that is worthwhile.

Ben continues thinking about his next step and what that should be. Time goes by, and Ben continues to sit on the balcony deep into his own thoughts. Then he almost has a revelation.

"That's it," Ben says, standing up and walking inside the apartment.

Once inside, Ben looks around at his apartment and at all of his possessions. There really isn't all that much: a couch, a television, a bed, and a few articles of random furniture. *Nothing that couldn't be replaced,* Ben thinks to himself. Standing there sizing up the apartment, Ben is ready for anything at this particular moment. A knocking at the front door brings Ben back to reality, so he runs to the front door and unlocks it. "Come in," he yells out, walking back to the living room.

Chase enters the apartment. "Hey man," he says in very calm and quiet tone. "How are ya?"

"I'm great. I'm great man," Ben answers the question rather confidently. "I've been thinking about all kinds of shit all day, and I've decided I'm not gonna be depressed and sad."

Chase, with a bit of amazement in his eyes, smiles and says, "Well, okay then." Chase then throws his hands up in the air and gets a small goofy look on his face. "So what's up? Why so happy all the sudden?"

"I've pretty much been drinking the day away, and I made a very unified and informed decision," Ben is all smiles.

Games Without Frontiers

"So you're drunk and you decided to ...?" Chase's voice trails off a bit towards the end of the sentence.

"I'm not drunk." At the very moment Ben says this, he lets out an enormous hiccup. It takes Ben a few seconds to catch his breath and continue speaking. "I'm gonna move. I'm gonna sell all my shit and move."

"Whoa, whoa, wait. Where are you gonna move?"

Chase doesn't give any time for Ben to answer. "Why sell all your things. Whoa, man, hold on. Let's think about this for a minute."

"There's nothing to think about. I'm gonna do it." Ben is very sure of himself even though he's slurring his words." I'm gonna move out to California."

"Where in California?" Chase asks unsurely.

"Where else? Hollywood!"

"So you're gonna sell your shit and move to California?"

"Yep."

"Are you fucking crazy?"

"Nope."

"Well, since you've given it so much thought, I think you should go." Chase looks up at Ben. "I mean, what have you got here keeping ya?"

"Nothing," Ben responds, a little shocked that his friend is so open to this idea and not ridiculing him for being spontaneous because he is drunk. "Really?"

"Yeah, I mean what do you have to lose?"

"That's what I've been thinking. I mean, things aren't really working out too great here." Ben's now really happy that Chase stopped by the apartment. "I just can't think of anything better to do with my life at this point."

"I agree, then I guess that's settled." Chase sits down on Ben's living room couch. "Do you need any help with any of this?"

"No, I think I'm gonna do this all on my own."

"I'm here if you need anything – any help, anything."

"I know that." Ben looks at Chase and then gives him a small hug with one arm. Ben doesn't mention anything about the fact that there's really nothing Chase can do to help, but the offer was genuine and that meant something. "Thanks buddy. You're a good friend."

"You're damn right I'm a good friend. You start talking all this crazy bullshit, and I'm right on board with ya." Chase laughs and then Ben begins to laugh with him.

"You're one crazy son of a bitch is what you are," Ben tells Chase, patting him on the shoulder. "You wanna come with me?"

"Hell yeah, but you know I can't."

Games Without Frontiers

"Why not?" Ben says aloud, then wishing he hadn't.

"You know why." Chase holds his hand up. The scars around his thumb are all very visible, almost like something out of Frankenstein in a way. "You know that I can't put any pressure on this hand, so therefore I'm pretty much useless."

"Don't ever say that." Ben takes a very serious tone. "Don't you ever say that."

Chase takes his attention away from his hand and smiles at Ben. "You know I'll always be there if you need anything from me. You're a great friend."

"No, I'm not," Ben says embarrassed a little." I'm a piece of shit who has no idea what to do with his life."

Chase takes a moment, and then looks at Ben straight in the eyes and says," Go to California."

9.

June 10's

It's hot as hell, and Paul is sweating his ass off. There's nothing like the desert heat. Sometimes Paul looks up at the searing sun, but all he can see is gleaming light so bright, it nearly blinds him, even underneath his shades. Paul sits alone on a bench, completely spread out with his helmet underneath the back of his neck. It's not exactly comfortable, but it's nice just sitting there for a few minutes. Sitting, spread out, he looks at his watch to see the time, and it's only mid-morning. "Shit, it's hot out here," Paul says aloud but no one is around to hear.

Paul was briefed shortly before this little break and is not looking forward the night at all. Paul's squad will be the lead sniper cover in a snatch-and-grab operation later that day. The operation isn't scheduled to deploy until midnight. So killing a little bit of time seemed like a good idea before he checked all his gear.

Games Without Frontiers

His squad will be landing on top of the extraction site, which is a large run-down building, and securing the operation from the roof – basically giving sniper cover and making sure no one escapes from the roof while the ground troops secure the building and their prisoners.

There is supposedly going to be some major players in the terror threat inside the building, so this was going to be a big night. Paul was not really thinking about the night. It was basically just another day and another operation to add on to the countless amount of operations that he was already getting used to. Same old shit, different day.

A smile comes across Paul's face for moment while he sits thinking about tonight's operation, almost as if he was realizing something for the first time. "This is gonna be good night."

Paul looks at his watch again and then gets up and starts walking to the base. There is music playing over the sound system throughout the base. It's Guns N Roses, one of Paul's favorite songs, he sings, "take me down to the paradise city."

Before he can get too far, he hears a voice call out, "Sergeant."

Paul turns to look and see who is calling out to him. Running up to Paul's side is Parker. "Hey hold up for a minute, Sergeant."

"What the fuck you want?"

"Hey, I just want to talk to you for a minute!" Parker hollers out to Paul, steadily getting closer.

"Look man, I just want to talk to ya, man to man, okay?"

"I'm listening." Paul continues to walk without hesitating.

"Look, man, slow down." Parker gets in front of Paul to stop his pace.

"I just want to speak to you for one sec, okay?"

"What?" Paul stops walking and turns all his attention to Parker.

"Hey, I just wanna say that I'm sorry for whatever it is I did to piss you off," Parker starts in. "I'm saying, I just want us to start over."

"What am I, your fucking woman?" Paul hisses. "You want to, like, hold my hand or something and sing a song."

"Look," Parker says, sucking up his breath and trying to not let his emotions come pouring out on Paul. "Is there any way we can just be cool?"

Parker gets no answer from Paul, who is looking at him with absolutely no emotion.

"Come on," Parker says, shrugging, trying his best to stay cool.

"What the fuck you want from me, Parker?" Paul wants to get the conversation over as quickly as possible.

"Look man, I know we don't see eye to eye on a lot of things," Parker is trying his best to be reasonable. "Look, I know we're on the roof tonight, and that means that we're gonna have to watch each other's ass."

Games Without Frontiers

Paul hesitates for a moment before saying anything. "Look, Parker, I don't know what it is you want me to say."

"I'm just want to talk to you for a second."

"We're talking."

"I know, man. It's just like, you know we don't see eye to eye on everything, and I just want us to get along." Parker stands quietly after stating this to Paul.

Paul is at a total loss of words.

He has no idea how to appease Parker, so that Parker will just leave him alone. "Parker, tell you what: tonight I got your back on the roof. Don't worry about anything else. Just don't worry about it. I got ya." Paul pats Parker on the shoulder.

"Man, you know, I just want to turn over a new leaf."

"Oh, I know, Parker." Paul withdraws his hand and lowers it back to his side. "And I know you went to the captain behind my back, you stupid fucking ..."

Parker interrupts, "You stupid fucking what? Say it. Say it, motherfucker." Parker's face is directly in front of Paul's. "Say it, you fucking chicken shit."

"Parker, you are speaking to a superior officer, so get the fuck out of my fucking face," Paul sternly yells, getting right up in Parker's personal space. "You got that?"

Parker backs away from Paul and stands at attention.

"Yes, sir," Parker salutes and stands there at attention as Paul walks off, not saluting back. "Look, Sarge, I went to the captain and told him about some of the shit you've been doing."

Paul turns around in much disgust and says, "You what?"

"You heard me, Sergeant. I went to the captain and told him about the bullshit you been doing on the side out here."

"You little fucking, snitch. What the fuck is the matter with you?" Paul is turning red in anger. "You little chicken-shit cock sucker. Who the fuck do you think you are?"

"Look, I'm done with your fucking bullshit. I tried to be reasonable with you, tried to be your friend." Parker is getting angrier by the second as well. "You're a fucking racist. I hear your stupid jokes behind my back. I'm not stupid motherfucker. I hear just fine, and you better believe if you said that anywhere else—"

"You what?" Paul interrupts. "Kick my ass, fucking pussy."

"You're god damn right. I'm sick of this bullshit." Parker is ready for Paul to take a swing at him, but neither man makes any kind of movement. They stand there looking one another in the eyes, sizing each other up, both ready for anything from the other.

"You wanna go behind my fucking back and be a snitch, you fucking piece of shit?" Paul starts to back off a little. "You don't know shit."

"Fuck you. I know enough, partner." Parker starts backing away. "I know enough."

Games Without Frontiers

"Look, look, hold on." Paul calms down a little and begins to reason. "Look man, if you want in on this shit, I'll cut you in."

"Man, I don't want nothing to do with that shit," Parker says under his breath, walking off.

Over the last several weeks, Paul made friends with one of the locals, steadily the local man started selling Paul marijuana and heroin, which he would then sell off for a profit. He was making a nice little extra wad of cash, which he hid from everyone, secretly stashing all the extra money away in his foot locker. Somehow, Parker must have found out about it, which made Paul very nervous. "C'mon, Parker. What the fuck?"

"Look, I tried motherfucker, and that's that." Parker doesn't even turn to Paul as he speaks, just gradually starts trailing away. Before he gets too far, Parker turns to Paul, who is right on his back and says, "Look, we're both going before the captain in two days, and we'll sort all this shit out then."

Paul stops following Parker and stands in one spot while Parker continues on his way.

"Parker, fuck ..." Paul's voice trails off a little. Paul stands for a moment, thinking, and then finds his way to his cot and his footlocker. Paul sits on his bed for a second and then turns to the footlocker on the floor in front of the bed. He looks through his things stacked neatly in a pile till he finds the bottom of the somewhat-small trunk.

Tucked in back, beneath everything, is whole bunch of Afghans and cash rolled up in to a little pile. Paul looks at the small fortune for a second and then stashes it back in its place. Paul puts everything neatly back into order and mutters ,"Fuck him," while situating the items in the locker. The only thing he keeps in his hand from the footlocker is a calling card.

Paul locks up the locker and makes his way to the phones. He punches in the calling card number and then dials Erin's number, which he knows by heart. There's a long array of clicking noises over the phone as the call is routed from the Middle East to America. The line begins to ring, finally, until the answering machine picks up.

"Hey, this is Erin. Leave a message." Then the loud answering beep.

"Hey baby, it's me. I just wanted to call you—"

The line suddenly picks up." Hello–hello?" Erin's voice has a small echo when she speaks. "Hey I was just thinking about you–thinking about you."

"Yeah, I was just thinking about you too."

"I miss you."

"I miss you, too."

"What are you doing?"

"I'm about to get ready. We're going on a run tonight. I'm not real excited about it."

"When are you ever?"

"Right."

"You know that I love you right?"

"Yeah."

"Everything's gonna be fine. I promise." Erin's voice is calm and at ease, which makes Paul feel euphoric, but only for a moment.

"Thanks, baby. I'm gonna take out the trash tonight."

"What, baby?" Erin sounds very confused.

"Oh, nothing. Just thinking about tonight." Paul begins to grin a little.

"You be careful."

"I will. I gotta go, okay?"

"Okay. I miss you."

"Miss you too." Paul hangs up the phone and then goes back to his bunk and starts to gear up for the night, thinking to himself the entire time about how the entire operation would go. Knowing that he would be alone on the roof with Parker for a few minutes, an opportunity might pop up.

10.

June 10's

Ben was only in Los Angeles a few months, and he was desperately learning to keep the pace of work life. Ben's personal life was more or less nonexistent. He was constantly working and never really had much time for anything but sleep. Tonight after work he planned to meet up with some friends he had recently met on the set of a large untitled film which was about to go into post-production. Ben was working as a production assistant on the untitled film; his job was very simple, the lead actor of the film, Nicolas, was in need of special security for his belongings, so Ben somehow fell into the spot.

So every day, Ben would show up to a studio on Lot C, check in, and then Ben would sit in a small room with a very large refrigerator unit, almost five hundred pounds or so, and guard the refrigerator so no one would get into it.

Games Without Frontiers

The reason for this was that the lead actor, Nicolas, liked to stay in really good shape while filming, so naturally he would look good and physically fit during shooting, which just so happened to be an action film with lots of stunts – although it was still untitled, it sounded like it was going to be really cool.

The refrigerator was full of extremely expensive caviar flown in from across the globe, which was the only thing Nicolas would eat while filming. The caviar was very high in protein and was actually quite filling, so Nicolas could eat all he wanted and never gain a pound of anything except muscle.

Ben would sit for twelve hours a day in a small uncomfortable chair next to the ice box, making sure that no one stole any of the expensive caviar out of it. The job was extremely boring, but it was a paying job, and Ben kept telling himself, "Everyone has to get their start somewhere." Even if this was a feeble job, it would most likely land him another job on another set. Ben kept his head up and his mouth shut, never complaining on the emptiness of his work or about how boring it would get sometimes. He showed up on time and never complained, which made him a semi-trustworthy individual to the others who met him on set.

Always being friendly was slowly paying off. Ben was meeting new people all the time: other crew members, actors, assistants of all shapes and sorts. Knowing people and having a good reputation was something Ben would not allow himself to fail at.

Names are kinda a big deal in this town. They could literally mean life or death to a project.

Today was Ben's last day on this particular job; next week he was to be an extra on a cop television-show pilot. His favorite job had somehow become standing in front of the camera. There was a feeling of excitement at being on screen instead of just pointing out your name in the ending credits. Ben had acquired an agent a few months ago who was slowly but steadily getting Ben work on different projects.

Mostly as walk-ons or maybe small parts with a line or two. Since Ben was once very much into acting, he fell very naturally back into it with the on-screen jobs. Working behind the camera was grueling work, which Ben was now getting accustomed, yet it was not as fulfilling or well-paying as it was for the actors who were on screen.

Both jobs were hard, but Ben was feeling much more comfortable doing on-screen stuff. Acting came naturally to Ben. He was good at it when he was younger, and he had only grown better at it with age. After a few acting workshops and some seminars, Ben was very excited at the pace his life was going, even though it was extremely difficult to be so busy all the time. Ben stayed continually hungry for it, never getting burned out or letting things get to him. He lived in a apartment, alone, and even though he wasn't there all that much, the rent was well over a thousand dollars a month.

Games Without Frontiers

Ben strung by doing all kinds of jobs to pay the rent and his bills – the higher cost of living was something else he was adapting to.

Ben was on the last chapter of the new Palanuik book, which was actually very good and made the time go by so much faster, when shift change came along. It was almost six o'clock and Ben's relief was already there. Ben decides to go to the Unit Production Manager and lets him know he was heading out for the day. The UPM Louie, a fast talking, no bullshit kind of guy asks, "Hey Ben, you coming to the wrap party tomorrow night?"

Turning to answer as he signs the sign-out sheet, writing his name and the time and then getting Louie to initial the sheet.

Ben looks up and says," I don't know, man. I'm actually meeting tomorrow night with a casting director on some new pilot. I maybe reading for the lead."

"All right then. I'll give you a call if I get anything for ya as well, buddy." Louie who hardly ever smiled, let a slight grin slip, for he genuinely liked Ben and enjoyed working with him.

"Later boss." Ben waves, exiting out of the office and holding the door open for a couple other crew members coming in behind him. It takes Ben about fifteen to twenty minutes to get to the bus stop. He stands there waiting for the next bus, which should be there in about five minutes. While waiting, Ben walks to a pay phone sitting close to the bus stop.

He dials his message machine number and checks his messages.

His friend Tom, who is also a working actor, has left a message saying, "Ben, its Tom, we're at the Scout Bar in downtown. Meet us here by nine."

Ben deletes the message after listening and, right about that time, his bus shows up. Ben pays the toll and walks back to a small empty spot on the already packed bus. While standing there looking around a bit, Ben can't help but overhear a couple of women talking. They're both Spanish and speaking in Spanish, and Ben understands only a word or two they are saying. Ben can overhear some things that sound as if the women are excited about something. They actually start speaking faster and faster the more excited they get, making it impossible for Ben to understand what they're saying. So he tries his best to ignore them, even though they start speaking to another person on the bus standing directly next to him, who is also Spanish.

The Spanish guy next to Ben starts getting excited as well when he starts speaking to the women. Ben is very curious as to what is going on and why everyone has started to jump around for joy. By the time the bus pulls to his stop, Ben can't wait to exit the bus, because the other passengers are getting so loud.

"Damn," Ben mutters to himself, exiting the bus and walking to the Scout bar.

Games Without Frontiers

As Ben enters the relatively small bar, he's surprised to see it packed on a weeknight. Everyone has their eyes on the television, even the staff.

No one seems to be paying any attention to much else. The whole bar is in high spirits, yelling, shouting all kinds of things like, "I can't believe it," or "This is amazing," and even a few *fuck yeah*'s are shouted at full volume.

Ben sees Tom across the bar, in a back corner at a small table with two other of their friends, Bobby and Reilly. Ben motions to his friends and then makes way through the crowd to their table. "Hey guys," Ben barely gets out when Tom holds up his hand and politely makes a gesture that means Ben should hold on a second, as he stares directly at the television. Ben gets somewhat comfortable and can hardly see the television, which has "Breaking News" sprayed all over the anchorman talking.

Ben, still not focused on what everyone is staring at, tries to make a quick gesture to the cocktail waitress, who walks slowly by, completely ignoring him, also staring at the television. Ben finally gives in and starts paying attention to what's happening on television. He can hear the anchorman, Anderson, saying, "All early reports to the situation are still not in so we are not yet able to confirm the death."

After hearing about the death, Ben says in a very moderate voice, "Who's dead?"

Reilly looks directly at Ben and says, "They finally got the fucker."

Ben, now with genuine interest, asks, "They got who? Who did they get?"

No one answers, but Reilly points directly to the screen.

"They think they got him."

Ben read's the little words floating across the screen, one by one. The words say, "World's most wanted man has been found and killed." Then Ben can hear the anchorman. "It seems an operation in the early morning hours has led to his capture and death. Hold on. I'm getting some new information." Anderson holds his ear for a moment, listening to something in his ear piece.

The entire bar is dead silent, waiting on the tips of every word. Total silence, as Anderson listen's to his ear piece, saying, "Uh-huh, uh-huh," then pausing for a second. "Well, ladies and gentlemen, this is proud day for the entire world, and we're now calling it the shot heard around the world referencing the first shot's in the American Revolution, symbolizing the hope of freedom from oppressors. In the early morning hours today, a marine unit infiltrated a top secret location, the location of which is being withheld at this moment, and we understand and are now confirming the capture and death of Osama—"

The entire bar roars, yells and screams everywhere. The bartender announces, "a round of drinks on the house."

Games Without Frontiers

People are hugging and dancing around – a very exciting moment for everyone.

Ben, feeling a little stupid and still not fully understanding the situation, asks, "What the hell is going on?"

11.

June 10's

Paul lays in the infirmary on a bed with his foot propped up in a newly fashioned cast. He is still on quite a bit of drugs administered by his doctor and nurse. Paul takes a couple of deep breaths and looks around the room a bit. There are soldiers all over the place for different reasons, mostly guys who caught shrapnel from an explosion or a gunshot wound. Paul really can't feel much and is barely awake. He lies there for a few a minutes, just trying to figure out where he is, slowly realizing that he'd been shot.

The little button is lit on the control panel next to Paul on the side of the bed. He pushes it for another wonderful dose of morphine. Paul is more or less quiet, not saying anything, not moving around much, compared to a few of the men who are screaming in pain. The noise has become so constant, that no one really hears the aches and groans. Paul looks around a bit, somewhat coming out of a haze.

Games Without Frontiers

Everything is getting clear for a moment. From out of nowhere, Paul hears, "How are you feeling soldier?" in a nice calm voice.

It's one of the doctors who Paul's seen a few times but never spoken to.

Paul looks up at the doctor and groans,"Hey, it's all in a day's work. I'm a soldier of the apocalypse." The doctor actually seems amused by the stupid little comment and picks up a chart next to Paul's bed and begins writing.

"How's your memory?" the doctor asks.

"I don't know what you mean." Paul is genuinely confused by the question.

"How about, what's your name? Can you tell me your name?"

"Ummm, it's Paul."

"Good, good, Paul. Do you know what day of the week it is."

"Uh, Friday?"

"Paul, do you remember why you're here?"

"I got shot in the foot. It really hurt."

"Good. Not good that it hurt, but I'm glad you're coming around. A few hours ago you told me you were just a pimp trying to make a living."

"No, I didn't," Paul says, laughing a little.

"Oh yeah, you wanted me to understand that pimping was in fact not easy, but always necessary."

"Oh man." Paul blushes a little in embarrassment.

"We're just glad that you're feeling better now. You had quite a night, hero."

"Hero? What are you talking about?"

"You'll see, son. I'm gonna let your captain know that you're feeling better. Okay?"

"Okay, I guess." Paul is very unsure what exactly is going on.

His memory starts slowly coming back to him. He can remember being lowered down from the helicopter and then jumping onto the roof. Parker and he were on the roof alone, until the stairwell opened up, and the enemy came out, blasting everything. It was the perfect opportunity for a shot, and Paul fired.

"Oh, shit," Paul mutters aloud.

The doctor looks down swiftly at Paul. "Everything okay, son?"

"Yeah, I just kinda had a flashback. I was on the roof with Parker."

"Well, okay then. Since the cap' wants to talk to you so bad, I'll tell him you are awake."

"Oh, sir, I don't know." Paul franticly tries to stop the doctor from walking away.

"Don't worry, son. Everything is gonna be just fine."

The doctor walks away. Paul feels anything from just fine. He is sick to his stomach. Paul almost throws up.

Captain Gualts is approaching steadily from across the room.

Games Without Frontiers

"Oh shit," Paul whispers to himself.

Gualts is in his early forties, big guy, very intimidating. Paul remembers in the back of his mind, not saying anything, that he and Parker were to have a sit-down with the captain, but due to the circumstances they were now unable.

Gualts approaches next to the bed and puts his hand on Paul's shoulder and give it a firm squeeze. "How ya feeling, son?"

"Sir, better, almost ready to get back out there."

"Good, son. Good." The captain sits down next to Paul at eye level. "So, son, what do you remember from the operation?"

"I was on the roof. We caught fire, and then returned fire."

"Okay, good." The captain, still eye level with Paul, is very interested in what he has to say. "So you returned fire?"

"Yes, sir. A small group of men came hauling ass through the door on the roof, and we were receiving fire from inside the building."

"So you opened fire when the enemy came through the door on the roof?"

"Yes, sir, it was so quick. Parker dropped, and I moved in from behind him and fired on the enemy. I think I dropped all three of them."

"You think?"

"Sir, they were no longer moving, so I rushed to Parker. He was laying there with blood all over his face.

I think I called for a medic. At around that time, I felt the shot go through my foot. I dropped and returned fire on the men. I guess I missed one of them."

"So you executed all of the targets?"

"Sir, yes, to the best of my memory."

"And Parker was shot before he could get a shot off?"

"Sir, the door flew open, and he spun like a top through the air. I wasn't doing my job. It's my fault."

"Don't be too hard on yourself, son. Shit happens. We all know that."

"Sir, it's my fault. He got shot because of me."

"No, he got shot by those stupid fuckers. You remember anything after firing on the enemy, Rambo?"

"Sir, they all dropped. I figured Parker was K.I.A. He was gasping in blood, and after I fired on the group a second time, they all went down – no more movement. The pain in my foot was excruciating. I looked over and some of the guys in my squad were rushing towards me. Next thing I remember is waking up here."

"Somebody was looking over your shoulder."

"Sir?"

"Not only are you hero, you got a million-dollar wound."

"Sir?"

"Well, son, the bullet went in and out of your foot, just about at your Achilles tendon."

Games Without Frontiers

"Your gonna need therapy to walk on it, but you will never be able to put much pressure on it, other than that. So the good news is your fight is over, and you're returning a goddamn hero."

"Sir, can I ask why you keep calling me that?"

"You'll find out all the details in time, but you're gonna reap the reward for the Ace of Spades."

"Sir, what happened to Parker?" Paul needs to know this information.

"Son, he's in a coma. He got a bullet through an artery in his neck. He most likely won't finish out the week, but his sacrifice was for something." The captain finishes and walks away from Paul.

Paul lies in the bed, wondering what exactly he'd done for the captain to call him a "hero."

Paul gets a big smile on his face and says to himself, "Not only am I a hero, I'm going home, and that fucker's never getting up."

Even though he wasn't exactly sure what was going on.

12.

July 10's

Ben was having a really bad day. The night before, he had stayed up late with no sleep, thanks to his upstairs neighbors who were having sex so loud Ben could hear every detail. What was scarier was the mental images that kept popping into his head. They weren't exactly the best looking couple on earth. He'd seen them a few times before in the hallways of the apartment building. The guy was super skinny, pale as the day he was born. He was always super trashy looking and almost never wore a shirt, so everyone could see his disgusting nipple ring, which was always swollen. The girl was missing two front teeth, probably from the crack pipe. She was all stringy and worn out looking all the time. Ben still wasn't a hundred percent sure she wasn't in fact a man with a golden blonde wig.

So after listening to dumb and dumber exchange all night, nearly banging a hole in his ceiling due to the sexual Olympics they were performing.

Games Without Frontiers

Ben really hadn't gotten even one good of hour of sleep.

There were a couple of important things to look forward to today.

Ben had an audition at ten and another one at three. This was the first time he had ever had two in one day, which was exciting and very stressful at the same time. The first one was for a new sitcom and the second was a small supporting role in a motion picture. Both paid nicely, and it would be great to get either.

Ben was studying the first audition. There were two pages of a script, and his part was Marty, who was the comedic relief in the scene Ben was reading. Trying to memorize the lines seemed nearly impossible considering the previous evening, but Ben managed to get a grasp on both scripts and was feeling comfortable with his audition.

When he arrives at the casting office, there is literally a line about ten men deep in the main hallway in the building. There's a sign printed on paper taped to the wall that reads "casting," with an arrow pointing down the hall. It was nine forty-five, so Ben was on time. He walks up to the to a signup sheet. His name is printed on the sheet and the time next to it says ten o'clock, re-affirming Ben is at the right place at the right time. He finds a spot in the long hallway and studies his lines. All the men in the hallway look about five years younger then Ben, but he doesn't allow this to discourage him. He simply keeps his place and studies his lines.

The hallway isn't very large, so all the men are trying to make a small amount of space their own.

There is a television in the front of the office, which Ben can hear but not see. A news show is on, and everyone on the show was talking about the same thing. Ben listens to the television and reads his lines over and over. The anchorman on the television is talking.

"Today the sergeant will be returning home, and he'll have a busy week to look forward to, for he will be receiving a purple heart and the Congressional Medal of Honor from the president himself." Ben tunes out and looks back at his lines.

Two men standing close to Ben, looking at their script pages, start up a conversation. "What time you get here today?" one of the men asks the other.

"Oh shit, man, they had me scheduled for eight forty-five and still haven't called my name."

Ben looks down at his watch after hearing this. He begins worrying a little that he's not going to make his other audition. Ben starts to worry a bit more as more time passes and only three of the men who were there when he entered the building have actually gone in the room and done the audition. He knows if he's not out of this audition by one thirty, he most likely won't be able to make the second audition, forfeiting any chance he would have at getting the part.

Games Without Frontiers

After more and more time passes, it's getting to be one o'clock and still no one has called Ben's name. "Shit," Ben mutters to himself, and then walks to the front of the hallway where there is a receptionist. Ben very courteously asks the receptionist if he can use the phone.

The receptionist is a young pretty girl with tan skin, long dark-brown hair and a very friendly smile. She slides a phone that no one's using to Ben. "Dial nine to get out." She looks at Ben and then returns to her business.

Ben dials out and calls his agent Jamie. He gets his voicemail."Hey Jamie. It's Ben."

"I'm at the first place still, and I don't know if I can make it to the second; and I don't have any number to contact them – just the address. Can you help me out? Thanks."

Ben hangs up the phone and pushes it back over to the receptionist. "Thank you."

"You need to get a cell phone. Everyone has a cell phone. Why don't you?" She is still being friendly, smiling the entire time she is speaking to him.

"I had one, but it died, and I still haven't moved on in my heart," Ben jokes, flirting a little.

"Oh well, that's a shame, but sweetie," – she moves in a little closer towards Ben across her small desk – "I think it's time that you moved on."

"Good advice, thank you." Ben smiles and walks back to the hallway, where everyone is still just standing around like zombies. "Oh man," Ben says under his breath, looking at his watch again."Shit."

A lady comes out of the hall and yells out, "Jason." The guy standing across from Ben, who had been talking to the other guy about the television, raises his hand and makes his way down the hall. Ben goes back to his spot against the wall in the hallway and sits down against it, letting out a sigh.

Standing alone now in the hallway, with no one to speak to, the guy across from Ben points to the television and directs a comment toward Ben. "You following this shit?"

Ben looks up from the ground. "Not really. I'm just too busy these days to really follow anything news-wise."

"I just can't get over this shit."

"I mean, this guy is out on a routine mission and runs into, of all people, Osama, and then fucking kills his ass."

"Yeah, I heard about that about a month ago, but I really haven't been—"

"Guy's a fucking hero. His name's Paul something. This Paul guy was just a sergeant doing his thing, shit."

"Yeah, I heard something about a reward, and he's getting some kind of book deal or something." Ben really isn't involved in the conversation.

Games Without Frontiers

Ben's starting to get really upset that it's taking so long for someone to call his name. At this point he's been there for a while, just sitting, and now he was going to be running behind, which meant there would be no second audition. The guy continues to talk, but Paul really doesn't care what he has to say. He begins to start sweating a little, especially his hands. He was feeling more and more nervous by the second.

"Ben," the lady who has been calling out names yells across the hallway.

"That's me."

Ben hurries up to her, and she escorts him into the small room where there are two people already sitting, both with little clipboards in front of them, both men. After being led into the room, the lady who called out his name closes the door and tells Ben to stand right there, in front of them. There is a small camcorder pointing to the spot where Ben is standing. He was already nervous, and now all eyes were on him.

"All right, Ben," the lady says. "I'll be reading the part of Donnie, and you'll be reading Marty, so I'll start." She turns on the camera and sits down, and then starts saying Donnie's lines.

Ben takes a deep breath and starts doing his part as Marty. They go back and forth for a few minutes. Ben is impressed with himself, giving the audition his all.

About halfway through the reading of the lines, one of the seated men says, "Thank you." The casting lady gets up, turns off the camera, and walks to the door, swinging it wide open. She calls out another name on her list as Ben exits. He immediately looks down at his watch to see how much time he has until the next audition. It's exactly one o'clock.

Ben folds up the scripts in his hands and runs out of the building, not forgetting to wave to the cute receptionist on his way out.

Walking outside of the building, he sees that by some miracle there's a taxi letting some people out. Ben hurries to the taxi as the passengers slowly exit, hops in, and says, "Look man, I'll give you fifty bucks if you get me to Seventh Street and Knight in twenty minutes."

"I try my best, buddy. Gonna be very tight." The taxi driver is a slightly older man who looks Persian; his English isn't great, but good enough to understand fifty bucks.

"I will appreciate it so much man," Ben says, taking a deep breath after hauling ass to the taxi.

The taxi driver starts driving like a mad man.

Somehow, through some miracle, they make it to the destination with five minutes to spare.

"Oh man you saved me," Ben tells the driver as he exits the taxi.

Games Without Frontiers

He hands him twenty bucks and then counts out the rest of his money. "I have exactly forty-eight. Will that be okay?"

"Yes, my friend." The driver takes the money and then tells Ben, "Good luck." He must have seen Ben reading his lines over and over again in the back.

Ben runs full speed into the building and tells the receptionist, another cute young girl, "I'm here to audition for a part."

"Oh, I'm so sorry. Tamara called in sick today. They canceled the auditions and moved them to next week. Someone should have called you." She returns to her work after telling Ben the bad news.

"Well, fuck," Ben almost says out loud but manages to keep it under his breath. Then he turns around and exits the building. There is a bus stop that is kinda close. Ben walks to the empty bench and sits down. In his mind, Ben keeps telling himself, "You can't give up. It's just a snag in the road. Don't give up. You made it here don't give up."

A small tear runs down his left eye. He wipes it the second he feels it so nobody will see it.

13.

July 10's

Paul's foot is itching like crazy, but since he has a big-ass cast on it, he looks everywhere in the dressing room for a wire hanger. "What's the point of having a closet with no fucking hangers?" Paul looks everywhere in the small closet in his dressing room for something long and thin enough to scratch his foot. It's difficult to get around the room with a cast and crutches, but he's slowly getting used to them.

Instead of popping his head out the door and just asking someone for some help, he sits down and looks around in his pocket for his bottle of Zanex. He pops the lid up and swallows a few pills. Erin should be back in a few minutes, and she'll help him out when she gets back. So hopefully the Zanex will take the edge of his foot until then. This will be his third television appearance just this week.

Games Without Frontiers

Paul had been really busy since he got back to the states on a press junket set up by the United States army. This public relations tour would be the last duties of his service for the military and would be receiving an honorable discharge afterword. Everywhere he went, people were calling out to him and chanting his name.

The fame came so abruptly, Paul was still not fully prepared for it, but boy did he love it. Erin was by his side all the time since he'd returned, which could get somewhat annoying since Paul was getting advances from every single girl in his path. Erin, on the other hand, was not able to keep her hands off of Paul since he got back. She wanted to fuck like everywhere possible they went. Paul was fairly certain that she has some kind of bet with herself, to have sex in every possible scenario they were a part of. Especially cool was the quickie they pulled in the White House before meeting the president. He was very relaxed by the time he met Barack. It was one of the best moments of his life getting the Medal of Honor put around his neck by the president.

After the White House, Paul was scheduled to appear on what seemed like every single talk show on television. As soon as he got off his plane home, a guy named Gale met him at the airport and asked if he could represent him on the celebrity circuit. Gale was not the first to ask, but he was the only one who showed up in person to meet Paul, so that made him the right guy for the job.

Gale was a mid-forties, big fat guy, but he defiantly didn't move slow, that was damn sure. Gale was setting Paul up for all the interviews and appropriately showing Paul the ropes of celebrity life. One of the first things Gale told Paul, as his client, was not to answer any questions about his personal life and to keep all the questions for the talk shows. Gale explained that if he got caught saying something to some paparazzi, they might construe it some other way than what the comment actually meant. The last thing they wanted was bad press. Paul was a bona fide hero if there ever was one. That was the story everyone would be running with.

"Damn, where the hell is she?" Paul's foot is about to drive him crazy. He had to take care of the problem before speaking to Craig on live television, or he knew he wouldn't be able to take his mind off of it. Looking bad on television was a huge "No No," so Paul sticks his hand in the side of his cast, but it won't fit all the way to the spot that is killing him. Someone knocks on the door. Paul turns to the door. "Come in."

The door opens. A young guy with a headset on pops his head through the door and says, "Fifteen minutes, sir," and then closes it right after telling Paul his cue.

"Thank you," Paul barely says in time before the door shuts. "Jesus Christ." At this point, his leg is killing him.

Another knock on the door, but this time there is no wait for Paul to answer.

Games Without Frontiers

Erin opens the door and is followed by a man in a very nice suit.

"Hey, honey." Erin walks to Paul and gives him a kiss on the lips. "This is Marc, the author who's writing the book."

Marc extends his hand to Paul. "Hey, it's nice to finally meet you in person," Marc exclaims while they shake hands.

"Likewise, I can finally put a face to the mental picture." Paul lowers his hand. "Marc, just one second, man. I've got to talk to her for a second."

"Oh, absolutely." Marc moves back away from the couple into the corner of the room and crosses his hands. Marc stands in the corner silent, he's a a very intellectual looking guy but not without his charm.

"Baby, my leg is itching like hell. Do you have anything?"

Erin looks around the room and then into her purse.

"Oh shit, honey. Ummm." She digs through her purse, looking for something that isn't there.

"Maybe this could help." Marc reaches into his pocket and pulls out a nice big metal writing pen.

"Oh yeah, yeah, yeah!" Paul looks like a kid on Christmas morning reaching for the pen in Marc's hand. Paul grabs the pen, slides it into the cast and starts rubbing his leg with it, letting out a huge groan. "Oooooo, that's the stuff. You're a life saver."

Marc smiles.

"You're welcome. It's always good to be of service."

"Good man. So, Marc, you were saying over the phone something about needing to put a rush on the book?" Paul leans back in his chair and becomes very professional. Erin stands behind Paul, scratching the back of his neck, with her attention towards Marc.

"Yes, well, that's exactly why I flew up here to New York, so we could meet in person and hopefully over the next couple of weeks have some alone time, so you can rehash everything to me," Marc tells Paul and Erin. "I've been getting calls, and there is a production company that is very interested in turning the book – once it's finished – into a movie, but they want to go ahead and get things started as quickly as possible."

"They're going to make a movie about me?" Paul and Erin are completely wide eyed toward Marc. "Holy shit, baby did you hear that?"

"Oh my god." Erin is so excited she starts fidgeting around like she has no idea what to do, and then she gives Paul a big kiss. "Baby, they're gonna make a movie about you."

Everyone in the room is excited now, laughing, in high spirits.

"Yes, they want to make a movie out of it, and I spoke to Gale. He's going to help you with all the details." Marc pats Paul on the back." Tonight, after the show, could you possibly swing by my hotel so we can speak some more about this?"

Games Without Frotniers

"Oh, hell yeah." Paul laughs and extends his hand to shake once again. Marc shakes his hand one last time and heads for the door.

"We'll talk more tonight. Good luck for the show, and oh yeah, keep the pen," Marc finishes, and then leaves the dressing room.

"Can you believe this baby?" Paul looks Erin directly in the eyes. She is tearing up.

"I'm so excited, baby." Erin jumps into Paul's lap. They hug each other tighter than they've ever hugged before. "You are my hero." She plants another one right on his lips. "And my sex slave." She kisses his neck this time.

"I'm on in like five minutes," Paul says and nudges her off. "I'm not a machine, woman."

They both laugh. There's another knock on the door. "Who is it?" they both exclaim at the same time.

The guy with the headphones on pops his head in. "Are you ready sir, 'cause we need to get going that direction."

"Oh yeah, I'm right behind ya," Paul tells him and then props himself up. As he stands he turns to Erin one last time before heading out the door and smiles. "I love you."

"I love you, too," she says and blows him a kiss.

Paul acts like he catches the kiss and puts it into his pocket. He then makes his way through the door and follows the headphone guy down the hall until he is just off stage.

Headphones tells Paul that they're going to wait there until the little blue light turns on, and then he tells him not to be nervous because Craig is really good about making his guest feel very comfortable. This is actually a relief to Paul as he stands there off-stage behind the curtain. Beneath the little blue light is a television monitor so Paul can watch the show while he prepares to be called out, getting more and more nervous by the second.

Until, after a few moments, Craig starts talking about Paul. "Tonight's guest doesn't really need much introduction. He's a decorated marine, and he is responsible for the capture of the world's most wanted man. We are very pleased to have him on our show. C'mon out here, Paul. Ladies and gentlemen ..."

The little blue light shines bright all of a sudden, and headphones opens the curtain. The spotlight hits Paul dead on. Thunderous applause echoes throughout the room. Everything else is completely inaudible. Paul makes his way onto the stage, taking his time with the crutches, being careful not to slip.

Craig is standing about halfway between the guest couch and the curtain. When Paul gets near him. They shake hands. "Please take a seat," Craig motions to the couch, and then makes his way back to the seat behind a desk. The crowd is screaming and cheering extremely loudly. After both men are seated, the crowd eventually quiets down some.

Games Without Frontiers

"How you doing, Paul?" Craig asks now that audience isn't screaming.

"I'm good, man. How are you?"

Paul smiles in genuine excitement at Craig.

"I'm great. So glad we got ya here tonight, because I feel I have a solemn duty here, to do something." Craig looks directly at Paul, and Paul starts blushing a bit.

"Oh man, and what is that?" Paul questions Craig's comment, unsure.

"Well, sir, I just want to thank you from my red-blooded heart for the service you did for this country and the rest of the world for finding that piece of BLEEP and killing him."

Thunderous applause roars throughout the studio. Craig extends his hand to shake Paul's hand once again. The two shake again, then Paul looks out the audience and makes a "thank you" nod as they keep clapping.

"So, Paul, what's it like to hunt down the world's most wanted man?"

"Oh man, I was just doing my job. I mean, anyone else would have done the same." For some reason, a glimpse of Parker comes across Paul's mind.

"From what I hear, you actually didn't realize what you had done until you were laying in a hospital bed the next day."

"Yeah, and then it didn't even seem real. It's all really weird. It still hasn't sunk in all the way." Paul smiles and continues. "I just so happened to be at the right place at the right time." The interview continues, but Paul starts feeling a little sick to his stomach, so he keeps all the conversation on his part to a minimum. The time flies right by, and before Paul knows it, Craig is announcing a commercial break.

"Stick with us, ladies and gentlemen, for Blink 182," Craig finishes, and the lights go down for the break.

Paul gets up out of the guest chair, before he can walk off stage, Craig stops Paul one last time. "It was a pleasure. Thank you so much."

"You're welcome."

As Paul makes his way to backstage, his foot starts itching again.

14.

August 10's

Ben was having a drink. It was the first he had had in a while. He was sitting alone at the bar, in a local pub around the street from his tiny one bedroom apartment. He'd spent the whole day at a callback for a television show that at first sounded very promising, but when he showed for the audition they were so impressed with one of the actors that auditioned before him, it became clear Ben didn't have a chance of getting the role. This role was pivotal to Ben, he really needed a paying job.

When the audition was over, Ben returned to his apartment. On the front door of his apartment was an eviction notice, so he had thirty days to find a new place to live. Ben didn't even want to go inside of his soon-to-be ex-apartment, so he found his way to the bar across the street. Drinking his troubles away seemed, at this moment, the only thing to do. He was on his fifth beer, watching the television in the bar. It was on some celebrity story that Ben couldn't have cared any less about.

Ben was thinking hard about his situation, not sure what to do. He didn't want to go back home, but if he stayed he had no idea where he was going to live. It was all so depressing.

"Another one?" the bartender interrupts Ben's thoughts.

"Umm, this time can I get a shot of tequila?" Ben looks at the bartender with a look of extreme sadness. The bartender, otherwise oblivious, notices the look on Ben's face. The bartender reaches to a bottle of tequila and two shot glasses. He pours a shot for himself and one for Ben, and then slides the shot to Ben.

"This one's on the house." The bartender raises his shot glass up. Ben grabs his shot and touches glasses with bartender. They simultaneously take shots.

"Thank you." Ben puts the glass down and slides it back to the bartender.

"You're welcome. Always can tell when someone is down on their luck." The bartender makes a gracious half smile. He grabs the shot glasses and puts them into a sink behind the bar, then reaches for a fresh bottle of beer and pops the top with his bar key. "I'm gonna close your tab after this, okay, amigo?"

"I understand." Ben picks up the fresh beer and takes a swig. When Ben places the bottle back down on the bar, he looks up at the bartender and says. "Can I ask you a question?"

"Shoot," the bartender tells him.

"Before I get into details, my name is Ben."

Games Without Frontiers

Ben extends his hand for a shake.

The bartender meet's hands with him, and they shake. "I'm Juan."

"Juan, I'm kinda stuck in a shitty situation."

"What's up?"

"Well, I moved out here a while back, hoping to work on movies or TV."

"And at first I thought I was going to make it, but now I'm broke, homeless, out of work, and I really don't know what to do."

"You want to be in movies. A movie star, eh?"

"Yeah, but I really would just take any job at this point."

"Ben, what you need to do is ask yourself how bad do you want it."

Ben sits for a moment, thinking before he answers. "I love it, but I just can't seem to be successful at it."

"There are some things that I want in my life as well, but I know my limits. I know I just can't give up everything I've worked for to have success. I mean I own this place, and that's taken me my entire life."

"I didn't realize you owned this bar."

"I struggled for years, doing all kinds of work, anything, like you said, 'cause I knew one day it would pay off; but in your situation, hard work and luck don't follow always follow the same path. I made my own luck with years of hard work."

"Now I live comfortably. I have my family." Juan reaches into his pocket and pulls out his wallet, looks through it, and finds a picture. He shows it to Ben. "This is *la familia, me esposa* Esmeralda, *y* Jennifer, *y* Virgina, *me hija's*."

The photo is a snapshot of the family. Ben looks a little deeper into the photo. The family looks extremely happy. "I love them with all my heart. I would do anything for them." Juan puts the picture away back in his wallet. "Every time I feel like I don't understand God, I remember all the things he has given me. Then I feel better knowing that my life has been blessed with a healthy family."

"Wow, Juan, I just don't know what I've been blessed with."

"You are young, you are alive, and you have a dream. Some never know any of these things. Your life is your own. No one can tell you how to live, except yourself."

"I'm only living day to day by chance. I have to make a decision: live like this or give up and go for a normal life."

"You say that luck is what holds your future. This is what you believe?"

"Ya, I guess in so many words. I mean, I just have to be in the right place at the right time, I guess." Ben realizes that Juan is making more since, than he expected.

"If luck is determined by chance, then I suggest we take one right now."

"Okay."

Games Without Frontiers

Ben doesn't really know where he is going with all this.

Juan reaches into his pocket and pulls out a quarter. "This coin, I found on the ground, walking into the bar this morning." Juan hands the quarter to Ben. "Maybe it found its way through me, to help you. Wouldn't you say that's how luck works?"

"I don't think anyone really knows. I mean, it's all chance."

"Then, Ben, I suggest you take one."

"That's all I've been doing."

"You don't understand. At this moment, right now, right here. It's going to change your life."

"Okay." Ben says, still a little unsure where Juan's getting at.

"Heads, you stay. Tails, you go back home. What do you say?"

"I can't just do that."

"Why not?"

"You know what, fuck it. Flip the coin."

"The only thing I can say before I flip it is that you must honor the chance, or else you are breaking a promise to yourself."

"I think I understand. Flip it."

Juan takes the coin, flips it, catches it and puts his hand over it. "You ready?"

"Yes." Ben's eyes are locked on Juan's hand.

Juan lifts his hand up, and they both stare at Washington's face for a second. Juan looks up at Ben, their eyes lock.

"Well, I guess I'm staying here."

15.

October 10's

Paul didn't like Los Angeles much at first, but it was slowly growing on him. He had a big studio apartment that was rented out for him in Orange County. He was staying there on other people's dime, because he was going to be a creative consultant on the film being made about him. Not only was he given this nice place to stay, Paul was receiving a nice sum of money working as a military liaison. Paul was still having trouble with his foot though. The cast was off, but he still wrapped it in bandages. Sometimes the pain could be excruciating, so he was taking painkillers left and right. Walking on his foot was difficult, but Paul could do it none the less. He also had a personal rehabilitation therapist seeing him four times a week. Jace, a real nice young guy around Paul's age, helped Paul with walking exercises and low-impact cardio to help Paul get more comfortable with the constraint of his foot.

Today, Jace had already come and left during the morning, giving Paul the afternoon to basically do whatever.

Games Without Frontiers

He relaxes on the sofa in the living room and turns on the huge flat screen television, flipping through the channels with the remote in one hand and drinking a whiskey sour in the other.

Paul wasn't supposed to drink while on the pain medication – some of which was prescribed, some illegally bought from a dealer.

Paul's dealer, since he'd been out in Los Angeles, just happened to be a guy he ran into while doing the TV circuit. Pete was scoring drugs for someone else there on the show, and they just happened to meet, and it turned out Pete was a fan of Paul's and offered to get him anything he needed.

So over the last few weeks, Paul would have Pete drop by his pad and hook him up with all kinds of stuff: morphine, coke, uppers, downers, footballs, etc. Paul was expecting his visit anytime during the afternoon that day.

Erin is still asleep in the bedroom. She'd been up late partying with Paul and some other "new" friends. Paul can't find anything about himself on the television, so he turns it off and stands up slowly and steadily, still trying not to put a ton of pressure on his foot. Paul walks across the living room and into the bedroom, finishing his whiskey sour on the way and leaving the glass on a shelf in the living room.

Erin is lying on the bed under the sheets, still completely out. Paul sits on the edge of the bed close to her. He runs his hand through her curly, dirty-blonde hair and whispers, "Are you awake?"

"Humph, I just, another minute." She opens one eye and then shuts it again.

"Baby, you need to get up. It's like ..." Paul looks over to the clock to see the time. "It's almost four. You've been asleep for like thirteen hours. You need to get up."

"I don't feel good," Erin mutters into a pillow and starts to stretch a little.

"My stomach hurts."

"Do you think it's something you ate?"

"I don't know. I just feel sick." She picks her head up and then puts it right back down on the pillow.

"Can I get you something?"

"Yeah, baby, can you get me a glass of water? My fucking throat is killing me."

"Sure thing." Paul kisses her on the head and then gets up of the bed. He walks from the bedroom into the kitchen, grabs a cup, and pours water into it. Then, before going back into the bedroom, he pops a valium and takes a drink of her water. After the swig of water, he makes his way back to the bedroom but stops about halfway because the door bell rings. Paul walks to the intercom. "Who is it?"

"It's Pete," he hears through the intercom.

"I'm buzzing you in. Come on up." Paul presses the gate button and then walks to the bedroom.

Games Without Frontiers

"Hey baby, here's the glass of water." Paul hands Erin the glass . She takes it from him and takes a drink.

"Thank you." Erin takes another big gulp. "Who's here?"

"Oh, it's that guy I was telling you about, Pete. He's here to drop off some stuff." Paul rubs the back of Erin's head. "Do you want to meet him?"

"No, I look like shit. I'll talk to him some other time."

"Okay, baby. I'm gonna go talk to him." Paul gets up and grabs the bedroom door. "I'm gonna close the door while he's here, so we don't bother you, 'kay, sweetie?"

"Okay." Erin rolls back under the covers, and Paul closes the door. He walks to the front door and unlocks it. Paul sits back down on the couch, and there's a knock on the front door.

"Come in," Paul shouts through the door.

Pete enters the living room. He's dressed nice, as usual, in a dim purple suit – very tasteful and expensive. Pete looks like a male suit model most of the time, which is funny, because at one time he told Paul he *was* a suit model. Pete walks sharply across the room to Paul sitting and shakes his hand.

"Paul, good to see, ya. How's the foot?" Pete sits in a lounger across from Paul.

"It's fucking killing me, as usual. I can't get the morphine anymore, won't prescribe it, which sucks. You bring me some goodies?"

"Of course." Pete reaches into a pocket inside the coat of his suit and pulls out a taped up plastic bag and tosses it on the table. "That blow is fresh off the boat. Crème del crème. You'll love it. I threw some Demerol in there for ya."

"How much?"

"Three large." Pete's tone is always relaxed.

Paul reaches into his pocket where he has a rubber band on a wad of hundred dollar bills. He counts out the money and hands it to Pete.

"Thank you." Pete counts the money himself and then stick's it into his coat pocket, and then says, "Why no TV today?" He points out that the television is turned off. "Nothing about you on, ha-ha."

They both laugh.

"Well, you know I've got be going. Things to see and people to do."

"All right man. I'll call you next week."

"My phone is always on."

Pete makes his way to the door and let's himself out. "Later."

Paul opens the little baggie up and shuffles all the different things out on the table into some sort of organization. He grabs the little bag of blow and shuffles out a small amount onto the glass coffee table. Paul reaches for a credit card out of his wallet, also sitting on the coffee table, and makes a few small lines of coke. He bends down and takes a hit.

Games Without Frontiers

When he looks up from the table, to his surprise, Erin is walking around in her pajamas.

"You weren't gonna invite me to this party?" She smiles and sits on Paul's lap, and then bends down and takes a hit as well. When she comes up from the table, she starts French kissing Paul, and then moves back a little. "You know, I love fucking you when we do this stuff. You make me feel so good."

Then Paul leans down and takes another hit. "You're not so bad yourself, sexy." He leans in to kiss her. They passionately kiss. She grabs the back of his head, brushing through his hair, pulling his face tighter. The phone starts to ring.

"Shit, I got to get this. Gale said he would be calling sometime during the afternoon, about the whole movie thing."

"Then go and answer it. I'll just be here pleasuring myself," Erin tells Paul, who's trying to get up and get to the phone.

He limps over to the phone and picks it up. "Hello?"

"Hey, Paul, what you doing? It's Gale."

"Oh, nothing." Paul turns to Erin and sticks out his tongue. She sticks out her tongue back at him.

"I just wanted to tell you, next week, they would like for you to meet the producer, Joel, and the director, Michael. They want to have you there while they do some of the casting. It will help them a lot, just to get to know you a little."

"So they want to meet, and with any luck they may want you to hang around for a while, because they're going to start casting this fucking thing next week. The book is still on the top ten charts for seven weeks straight, starting tomorrow, so they want to get this whole thing moving A.S.A.P. You get me?"

"Have you heard anything from Marc since the book was released?"

"No, I told you, there's not going to be any more communication between you and him, other than friendly stuff, once the book debuts. He's got other stuff. I know you hate the title, but there's nothing we can do about that anymore."

"It's just, it's killing me that he named the fucking thing *Paul's Song* after I specifically asked him not to. Shit, it just pisses me off."

"Look, P money, that's just the nature of the business. You were his assignment. He put the work in, he gets to name the damn thing whatever he wants. I mean, look at it this way, he stayed completely faithful to your story and represented it with you looking nothing but good. Why worry?"

"I know, but "Paul's Song?" It just sounds so fucking stupid. Why couldn't he call it "The Shot Heard Around the World," like everyone else did? I mean isn't there already something called *Brian's Song*?"

"Don't sweat it, baby. You're money. Everything's gonna be gold with this deal. Don't worry about some stupid fucking title."

"I guess you're right."

"Tell that little wifey of yours I said hello, and no, she can't beat me in chess. I don't care what she says, all right. And I'll call you tomorrow around this same time. We can get together about the movie thing, I can kinda coach you through the basics, so you're not just standing there with your dick in your hand."

"That sounds good. I guess I'll talk to you tomorrow."

"All right, buddy. I will get back to you with the times and places. Don't be nervous about any of this. It's gonna be money, okay?"

"You're right, I guess." Paul is still pissed, but there's not much point arguing about it anymore. "I'll talk to you tomorrow. Later."

Paul hangs up the phone and turns to Erin. "I am meeting with the producer and the director of the movie next week. They're about to start casting, so I guess they want to kind of have me there. Hell, I should just play myself."

Erin looks up. "Have you ever acted in anything before?"

"No. You know that."

"I would leave that up to the big guys and not worry about it."

"It's not that I'm worried. I just don't want to get fucked on this whole deal. I mean, I hate the title of the book."

"You have a book about you. Why do you give a shit what it's called?"

"It's about me. It's my life."

"I should get a little more say in it, don't you think? Fuck them, if they think their gonna get some pussy motherfucking actor to play me, that for damn sure."

"Baby, come here." Erin motions for Paul to come and join her.

Paul walks to Erin.

"You are a fucking hero." She reaches up and grabs him and pulls him down to her level. "And besides, why do you give a shit what everyone thinks. They are the same assholes who have been jealous of people like us their entire life. Everyone loves you, especially me." She leans up to and kisses him. "Everything is gonna be fine. We're here; we made it this far. No one can take this away from us now. Who knows what will be next for us."

She always knows how to cheer him up.

16.

November 10's

Ben was sleeping on the couch at his friend Tom's apartment for a few weeks. Tom found out about Ben's trouble's and extended a helping hand, for he himself was also struggling actor but not as hard off as Ben. They worked out a way for Ben to help with the rent, so Tom was getting a little help with that while being able to give his friend a roof over his head. Another nice thing was the two could go to auditions and jobs together, because they were finding small jobs on lots of the same projects. Ben kept true to his promise to himself. It was also nice having a friend in the same boat, so there was a mutual respect and support for one another.

It's about seven o'clock in the morning, and Tom is already up getting ready. He has a walk-on role today for a big new television show called *Creatures*. Ben was planning to tag along, because he was offered a part-time job on the show, helping as a production assistant. Tom had a car, so they carpooled together to jobs.

"Hey bro, time to get up."

Tom looks down at Ben on the couch.

"Agh." Ben stretches and leans up, yawning. "What time is it?"

"It's just now seven. We got to be there by eight-thirty. It's only about twenty to thirty minutes from here, so we need to get going before eight. So get up."

"Yeah, yeah, I'm up, I'm up." Ben stands up, walks to the bathroom and washes his face and brushes his teeth. "I'm done. Let's get going."

They exit the one-bedroom apartment and make their way down to Tom's Kia. They drive to the studio lot, show their little passes to the security guard, and find a not-too-bad parking space for a change. Ben and Tom enter the lot together, but Tom heads off to where the casting call is being held, and Ben makes his way over to the unit production manager.

"Hey Lou," Ben says walking up to his desk.

"Ben, what's happening?" Lou hands Ben a headset. "I'll need you on three today to do some odd jobs – nothing too serious; just unloading and loading equipment. Today is actually going pretty well so far, so I'm hoping"– Lou crosses his fingers – "that it stays that way for the rest of the day."

"Where do you need me right now?" Ben places the headset on his head.

"Um, craft services is running a little behind. Can you go over there and give Jeff a hand with that."

"Sure. I'm on three, if you need me."

"Cool." Lou returns to his work, as Ben walks away. Ben makes his way down the hall to the break-room slash cafeteria, where he sees Jeff, a fellow P.A., putting together some tables.

Ben walks up to Jeff. "Hey, Jeff. You need some help with this."

Jeff turns around and looks at Ben for second, almost in confusion.

"Um no, sir. You just relax. Me and the assistants can take care of this."

It's not until he's finished that Jeff does a double take and realizes that he's gotten Ben confused with someone else. "Oh shit man. I thought you were someone else. Yeah man, I'm folding out these tables, and then I'm gonna unload the catering truck. Give me a hand with that?"

"Sure thing." Ben starts unfolding tables and pushing chairs up to them. The job goes much faster with the two of them doing it together.

"Here's the keys to the van. It's parked right outside up here on the left. Can you get it open and start grabbing the trays of food for down here."

Ben takes the keys from Jeff and makes his way down the hall towards the van. As he walks down the hall, a couple of young pretty girls walk by him and says very flirtatiously, "Hey, Paul."

He waves back to them, even though they have him confused for someone else. Ben props the building door open and walks over to the van. He opens the back and starts shuffling through the platters of food. While standing outside, he decides to smoke a cigarette, so he pulls one out of a pack in his pocket and lights it. He stands there for a moment smoking, when a young guy in a suit out of nowhere walks up to him.

"Hey," the young guy in the suit slaps hands with Ben. "Hey, later on today, can you holler at me and Joel. We really need to get you to take a couple a pics for us."

"Umm, okay." Ben continues to smoke and the young guy walks off. He finishes his cigarette and stacks some of the trays of food on top of one another, and then makes his way back inside to Jeff wondering if this an episode of *The Twilight Zone*.

"Great. Umm, just put those right here for now. I'll sort them as you bring them in." Jeff takes the trays from Ben and starts laying them out on the tables. Ben and Jeff continue this for about half an hour until all the food is laid out nice and neat for whenever they call "lunch."

Jeff looks at Ben. "Thanks for the help. If you want, you can go ahead and grab yourself something to eat."

"Awww, thanks man. I'm actually kinda starving." Ben picks up a Styrofoam plate and a cup and helps himself to some tea and a sandwich.

Games Without Frontiers

Ben sits alone at a table, eating his sandwich and drinking his tea. While he's sitting there, two guys walk into the room, both dressed nice. One is in his fifties and one looks Ben's age. The one that is Ben's age grabs a plate and helps himself to the food lying out, and then he sits across from Ben, alone, as the older guy leaves the room.

Ben can't help but notice that the guy sitting there eating looks very similar to himself. Both are around the same age, with dark hair and brown eyes. They even have the same facial shape.

Ben, trying his luck, speaks up to the guy. "Excuse me, sir."

The guy looks up at him. "Yes?"

"I'm sorry to bother you, but by any chance is your name Paul?"

"Yeah, it is. You've seen me on television, huh?"

"Oh man, I don't watch television, but I think some people here today have been confusing me for you. They've been calling me Paul."

"Really, that's funny. You know what, you do kinda look like me." Paul stands from his seat and walks to Ben. "I'm Paul."

"Yeah, I know ... I'm Ben." Ben laughs a little when saying this. They shake hands.

Paul looks down at Ben. "Umm, so what do you do around here?"

"Oh, I'm just a production assistant. I do this when I don't have any acting jobs."

"You're an actor, huh. Really?"

"Umm, yeah, kinda. Oh yeah, some guy in a really nice suit came up to me, I guess thinking I was you. He started calling me Paul and wanted you to meet with him and Joel."

"I bet that was his assistant, Brian. I was actually about to head that way after I ate something."

"I really don't know. That's all he said."

"But he thought it was me. That's pretty funny. I bet your were like, what the fuck, huh?" They both laugh.

"Yeah actually, I was a little lost, but at least I got to relay the message."

"I really appreciate that. They're actually casting someone to play me in a movie, and everyone's having a hard time agreeing with each other. I guess I'm a hard shell to crack or something."

"What's the movie about that you're making?"

"I haven't seen a script, but mostly I think it's about me."

"You look familiar. I'm sorry I don't know you."

"Hey, that's okay. It's actually nice having someone who isn't trying to kiss my ass left and right."

"How could you not like that?"

"Ha ha, so you act. Have you been in anything I've seen?"

"I doubt it. It's all bit parts on small shows, some of them never found their way on air."

"Well, don't sell yourself short. All I did was shoot a guy, and now I'm here because of it"

"Oh, that's it, the shot heard around the world, and all that. That was you?"

"Yeah. Crazy, huh?"

"Well, geez, man, I mean it's nice to meet you." Ben gives Paul a thumbs up. "Good job."

"Thank you."

Paul sits for a second in silence then says "I like you Ben. You're like one of the only real people I've met so far in this city. I like that." Around that time the older man in the nice suit that was talking to Paul earlier returns.

"Hey, Gale, you should meet this guy right here. His name is Ben."

Gale looks over to Ben. "Hello." He makes a small wave with his hand.

"Hi." Ben politely smiles.

Paul points to Ben and says," He looks like me doesn't he?"

Gale turns and looks closer at Ben. "Wow, he does look like you in a kinda-sorta way."

"Well, thank you, I guess." Ben's not exactly sure what he's supposed to be saying or doing.

"Gale, this guy's an actor, and he's stuck working as a production assistant."

Paul points this out. "I think he should come with us and do a read."

Gale looks at Paul as if he's joking, but Paul is dead serious. "Really ... well hell, why not." Gale directs his attention back to Ben. "You're an actor right?"

"Kinda." Ben's not as assured as he usually is, because he feels blindsided by the two men.

"Well, you are, or aren't you?" Gale uses his deadpan serious look which is very intimidating.

"Yes, sir. I am."

"Tell you what, Paul, why don't you grab your friend here and bring him back with us. Let him do a reading." Paul nods his head in agreement and then turns to Ben.

"What do you say? You want to come and do a read for the part of me?" Paul smiles, knowing he is offering a big chance to his new friend. Ben is almost in shock at this moment and hesitates for a moment before he answers.

"I would love to come with you guys, but I am kinda working right now." Ben doesn't want to just leave without telling anyone.

Paul looks him dead in the eyes. "Look man, right here, right now. What do you say?"

Ben slips off his headset and says, "Fuck it. Let's go."

Games Without Frontiers

"All right," Paul says, very excited. "Let's do it to it!" He gets up and motions to Ben to follow. "Are you ready for this?"

"I was born ready." Ben smiles finally sure of himself.

"Yes." Paul's still excited. "Here's the deal."

Paul starts walking down the hallway adjacent to the kitchen. Ben catches up and walks along his side. "They're looking for someone who looks like me and acts like me, so that's what you're going to try for, okay?" Paul puts his arm around Ben's shoulders. "I'll try my best to help you out."

"I can't believe this." Ben is almost hyperventilating. "Your awesome, man; this is great."

"I know, I know. Now, Ben, you're gonna have to calm down some, all right. Take some deep breaths." Paul continues to give him pointers as they walk together down the hall. "Look man, relax, just be yourself – as me, ha-ha."

"All right." Ben forces a small laugh.

"Ben, I think this is the start of a beautiful friendship," Paul tells Ben. "I'll pull for you, buddy, don't worry."

By the end of the day, Ben was offered the part.

17.

December 10's

Paul and Erin were home for Christmas this year for the very first time together. Erin went all-out buying everyone an expensive gift. Paul was too busy in the weeks before working on the movie, so he let her pick up all the gifts and he picked up the tab. Truthfully though, the only thing Paul was busy doing was getting fucked up. Their drug habit was beginning to get expensive, but he was managing to balance everything out. The movie people were paying him nicely for his work as a military liaison.

They go to Erin's mother's house to start the Christmas off. Tomorrow, they would be celebrating with Paul's family. Erin's mother, Linda, had been divorced from Erin's father for almost ten years. Sometimes he showed up for Christmas, but most of the time he didn't. So, to Erin's surprise Gregg, her father was at her mother's house. Gregg brought along his new girlfriend Shannon, who was just a bit older than Erin. The two were drunk most of the time. And when her father was blitzed, things usually got ugly.

Games Without Frontiers

Paul personally couldn't wait to get the whole thing over with. He would have to sneak around the entire time with the drugs he had with him – today with Erin's family and tomorrow, which was actually Christmas Day, with his own family.

Everything was okay at first. Paul pretty much stood his ground alone. Erin was busy off doing something with the rest of her family the whole time. Paul didn't really know anyone that well, but everyone sure knew him. Everyone was excited to see him. This was the first time home since he had became a nationwide hero. Erin had a big family that was also very close. Paul didn't, so it was all very new to him how to act around a room full of people that knew each other very well, and he didn't know anyone really except Erin.

Mostly the day was pretty cool. Greg and Shannon were wasted by the evening. Linda was so busy in the kitchen Paul never saw her very much. He spent a good deal of the day getting to know her family. Erin had brothers and sisters, aunts, uncles, grandfathers, grandmothers, nieces, nephews; there were all kinds of members of the family running around. Most of which, showed up just to meet Paul. Paul didn't really get to know anyone enough to remember their names, plus he was high as a kite the entire time. Paul made several special visits to the bathroom, and each one put Paul in a better mood.

After they had a big family dinner, the family opened presents. Paul let Erin open all the ones for the two of them.

Everyone opens the gifts from them as well.

The couple got many "thank you's" from all around. Their gifts were by far the most expensive given. Erin had picked out really nice presents to give to everyone, such as jewelry, big-sum gift cards, expensive electronics, etc.

Everyone was very pleased with their gifts, except for Paul.

As Erin opened each gift, he couldn't have been any less underwhelmed. They were given picture frames, a coffee maker, some ugly clothes, a cheap video camera, and lots of other items that Paul couldn't care any less about. Paul's favorite gift was a copy of the *Back to the Future* DVD's, and it was the only one he thanked anyone for.

Once the present-opening was over, Paul finds himself a spot outside in a lawn chair with a beer and a cigarette and sits alone, basically just killing time till Erin's ready to leave. Gregg comes and joins Paul, uninvited.

"Can I bum a smoke?" Gregg asks Paul.

"Sure." Paul reaches into his pack and hands Gregg a cigarette. He lights it for him.

"Thank you." Gregg slurs his speech a little.

"Yeah, no problem," Paul tells Gregg and continues to drink his beer in silence.

"Hey, Paul?"

"Yes, Gregg."

Games Without Frontiers

"Can I talk to you about something?"

"Sure."

"I hate to do this, but I'm trying to put something together out here. I've got this system I've entered into, and it's the real deal. I hate talking about money on holidays." Gregg lets up for a second.

"Well, then don't," Paul laughs as though he's kidding.

"Ha ha, right. Well, see, I've got this deal going, and it's really going to be sweet. I'm taking over these sells from my agent."

"You have an agent?"

"She's not really an agent. It's more like I work directly under her."

"Oh, well, she's your boss then."

"No, it really doesn't work like that. Let's just call her my agent."

"Okay."

"My agent has five clients, who move into the agent spot, and I'm one of the clients now, but soon I will be an agent."

"Okay."

"So we have these great deals we offer; like, let me ask you, how much do pay you for like say household apostasies?"

"I don't know. Depends on what it is, I guess."

"Okay, right. Well, let's say you want to buy a hundred-dollar coffee table. This company cuts out the middle man and gets the coffee table straight to you."

"Okay."

"See, it's actually very convenient. Instead of going to the store and paying full price, our service offers to give you the exact same item for a lesser price. Sounds great, right?"

"I'm listening."

"So you have all these items, you take them directly from the manufacturer at a discount and then sell it your clients for any even bigger discount for your agent, so essentially everyone is making money and saving money at the same time."

"I see."

"There's an initial investment, of five hundred, and then you're off making your own money. There's no catch"

"Okay. You want me to make an investment and then sell products under you to make a return on that investment?" Paul reaches down to massage his foot while he talks to Greg. It's beginning to hurt and make him feel uncomfortable.

"Well, no, you're not really listening to the whole picture. You make money by spending money."

"Gregg, can you excuse me for moment? I need to go use the bathroom real quick. When I get back, we'll talk more about this, okay?"

"Yeah, sure thing," Gregg smiles politely.

"I'll be right back." Paul stands up and walks inside to the bathroom.

Games Without Frontiers

Paul locks the door behind him and pulls out a small vial from his pocket. He lays a line of coke on the sink and snorts it.

There's little grains he missed, so he licks his finger so the white powder will stick to it, and then rubs it on his teeth. Paul turns the sink on and washes his face, then reaches into another pocket and pulls out a small pill bottle. He pops a couple of Vicodins and a Zanex. He takes a gulp of water from the running sink to wash the pills down. "All right." He leaves the bathroom.

Paul sees Erin in the kitchen, helping her mother wrap up leftovers and clean dishes. Paul enters the kitchen. "Linda, the food was great. Thank you so much."

"Well, you're welcome." Linda smiles at Paul.

"Do you mind if I borrow Erin for a moment?" Paul asks very politely and smiles.

"Sure, hun," Linda answers.

"Sweetie, can I borrow you for a moment?" Paul turns his attention to Erin.

"Yeah, babe. What's up?" Erin stops helping and walks towards Paul. He pulls her out of the kitchen into a corner of the house where they are alone.

"Look, we need to get the fuck out of here." Paul is extremely serious.

"Why, what's wrong?" Erin is genuinely surprised by the comment.

"Your fucking drunk-ass dad wants to try and get me to invest into some kind of Pyramid scheme."

"Don't call him that."

"What do you want me to call him?"

"Look, I know he has a problem with alcohol, but I'm sure he was just trying to be nice."

"No, he wants me to make money for him."

"Look, you don't have to be an asshole. Let me just go tell everyone bye, and then we'll get out of here."

"No, fuck that. Let's just go. I've already put our shitty presents in the rental car."

"Whoa, whoa. Why the fuck are you being so rude?"

"Me being rude? I'm not trying to suck your family dry with a stupid scheme that's not going to work. I'm the asshole, your right."

"Look, I'm not leaving till I say goodbye to everyone, okay?"

"Make it quick. I'll be in the car."

"You're such a dick."

"Look, I'm leaving. If you want to stay, then stay. I'm not."

"Fine, fine." Erin's getting upset and Paul isn't backing down. He turns away from her and heads out the front door, jumps into the car and then starts it. Erin comes out the front shortly after and gets into the passenger seat. She slams the door behind her, but Paul doesn't care. He wastes no time and starts backing the car out of the drive way and then hauls ass down the street.

Games Without Frontiers

Paul looks over at one point, and he can see that Erin is teary-eyed and crying. Paul ignores this and keeps driving for a while.

Neither says a word to one another.

After about an hour of driving, Paul finally speaks up. "Look, I'm really sorry. I'm just tired. It's been a really long day." Erin doesn't say anything. She just sits there quietly, acting as though she's ignoring him. "I'll tell you what. Let's just get a hotel room and take it easy for the rest of the day, and then we'll get up tomorrow and finish the trip, okay?"

"Whatever, I don't care." She couldn't be any less enthused.

Paul pulls off to a nice little tucked away Hotel Inn and rents them a room for the night. When they get inside of their room, Paul drops the bags down onto the floor into a pile, walks over to a night table and spreads out a line. He snorts it, and then looks up at Erin. "You want one?"

"No."

"Okay." He spreads out another line and does it. "That hit the spot." He smiles and lies down in the bed.

"Look, Paul, I really think you need to take it easy with that shit."

Erin sits on the corner of the bed with true concern. "I mean, you're doing it all the time."

"So?" Paul doesn't care much for her concern.

"Paul, I have to tell you something."

"I've been keeping it a secret, and I just didn't know when to tell you," Erin tells him. "We can't go living like this."

"I talked to my mom about it, and I think I'm gonna stay here for a while."

"What?" Paul sits up. "Are you leaving me?"

"No, I'm not leaving you. You're gonna be so busy with the movie thing, you aren't gonna have any time for us."

Paul looks at Erin directly into her eyes." What is going on here?"

"Paul, I'm pregnant."

18.

December 10's

Captain Dye was an asshole and Ben was hating every moment of boot camp. Well, it was actually celebrity boot camp. It was part of the deal when Ben was offered the part of Paul in the –project with the running title "Shot Heard Around the World." Captain Dye was a ranking army ranger, and he was the go-to guy for celebrities to learn about the experience of actually being in a war. Dye had worked on just about every single film that involved the military. Ben didn't realize what shitty shape he was in until he started this nearly impossible workout regimen.

Dye would wake Ben up in his tent out in the wilderness in the morning by firing some live rounds into the air, and then till about midnight Ben would work non-stop. Ben's duties and workouts were so exhausting, he barely could make it for one day, let alone three weeks of this shit. This was his fifth day of Captain Dye's regiment, and it wasn't getting any easier.

The good thing that was coming out of this was that Ben was learning so much about being a soldier. Dye was tough, and the tougher he was on Ben, the more Ben learned.

Ben had never fired a gun before, and now he was becoming a certified sharp shooter. Ben was firing live rounds at targets for a few hours every single day. Also Dye was teaching Ben combat skills and all kinds of crazy takedown techniques. As for the exercise, Ben was forced to wear a twenty-pound platelet around his shoulders, which made everything that much more intense.

Captain Dye started that day off, as usual, by firing a few shots off into the air to wake up Ben with gunfire. After this ordeal, Ben would eat a MRE for breakfast. After breakfast was the seven-mile hike with Dye on his ass the entire time, yelling and screaming all kinds of shit at him. Dye was teaching Ben all the standard operating procedures orally while he exercised. Another huge benefit from all of this strenuous activity was that Ben was getting into great shape. Ben could literally look down at his body and notice a small difference daily. This was the best shape he had ever been in, so this was one of the good things about all this.

Throughout the day, Dye would sneak off and fire some live rounds at Ben while he was training. Most of the time, it would scare the hell out of Ben, but now he was slowly getting used to the random shots fired.

Games Without Frontiers

One thing that was ringing in and out of Ben's mind during this ordeal was the fact that he could quit anytime he wanted. But every time he felt weak, he would reassure himself that it was defiantly worth it. This film was going to make Ben a star, and he knew it. Thinking of all the doors this opportunity was going to open for Ben was mesmerizing. He didn't really have much time to think about these things, but they were always a constant reminder when things got tough.

It was about halfway through the day and Ben was taking a small break to eat. During the break, Dye would yell things at Ben. On this particular day, Dye was starting to get kinda deep with his thoughts.

"You fucking maggot. You have any idea what it feels like to be at war?" Dye yells at the top of his lungs at Ben.

"No, sir," Ben answers swiftly and equally as loud.

"Your best friend dies, standing right next you. How do you feel?"

"Sad, sir," Ben yells.

"No, you stupid motherfucker, you don't have time to feel fucking sad, you fucking pussy. Get on your face and give me twenty-five."

"Yes, sir." Ben drops to the ground and starts doing pushups.

Dye stands over Ben and continues, "You feel glad. Do you know why you feel glad?"

"No, sir."

"You feel glad because it wasn't you, that's why."

"Yes, sir."

"So how do you feel when your buddy bites the dust?"

"Good, sir."

"Outstanding, now you're getting it. Now let's move. Get your ass up. We're going up the creak pass and then we're heading down into the mountains." Dye takes off running up the hill. That was the one of the longest conversations for the entire week.

"Yes, sir." Ben stands and gets going, Dye yelling at him every second of the way. Ben was hurting, but passion was keeping him alive.

Ben knew he could gut this out no matter what. He had waited long enough for this opportunity, and Ben wasn't going to blow it.

Running up the hill, with Dye shouting at him the entire time, Ben thinks to himself. Ben envisions a calendar and counts the days on it, in his mind. For a moment he staggers a bit, but then he finally comes to a conclusion that it is in fact Christmas Day. "Merry fucking Christmas," Ben tells himself, running up the hill. Once on top of the hill, Dye orders Ben to give him fifty pushups. Ben's arms are like Jell-O and he continues to push himself harder than he ever has before. "You can do this. You can do this."

After finishing the boot camp, Ben would acquire a new found confidence and strength that he had never possessed previously.

19.

March 10's

Paul was sitting inside his trailer, having his lunch which was a fifth of vodka and couple of painkillers. The trailer was sitting on the lot right next to the location where the movie was being filmed. They were in the middle of a small desert in Mexico. It had the right look in the director Michael's mind, and plus it was super cheap to film there. Paul didn't like it much. He had been expecting to film the movie back in L.A., but this was the location that was chosen, and as usual he had little-to-no say in it.

The only real triumph as far as creative involvement was the choice for Ben to portray him in the film. Nothing else was really his decision. The script loosely followed *Paul's Song*, which was already a verbal re-creation from Paul's memory of that night. The story the film was telling had very little to do with Paul's actual life. It was more of an inspirational piece of one soldier's courage against the odds. That was all well and good, just as long as Paul was put into a hero's light in the story.

Paul was even more pissed today than usual though, because apparently the producers had decided that Paul was a boring name, and they wanted to change it. So of course the name was going to be changed from Paul to whatever the producers decided they liked the most. Today was the third day of actual filming, and so far they hadn't shot any scenes with the character Paul. Now was the time to change it, before they wasted any film with this major creative decision.

The inside of Paul's trailer was actually pretty nice; there were two televisions, TiVo, a nice queen-sized bed, a personal kitchen, and somehow it still managed to be spacious and had plenty of room for people to join him inside. Right now, however, he was all alone, enjoying the time in the fresh cool air. Paul's foot was hurting more and more almost every day, and he was finding it harder and harder to walk. There wasn't really anyone there to help him with the pain, so he never really mentioned the fact that he was in a lot of pain to anyone.

The drugs and alcohol were becoming, more and more, a constant in his life. They weren't taking away the pain like they used to, so Paul found himself indulging more and more. This situation wasn't going very well on set though; everyone could tell when he was wasted. It affected his entire demeanor, and since he was becoming increasingly dependent to the drugs and alcohol, Paul was walking a very thin line with his work on the project.

Games Without Frontiers

His increasingly erratic behavior could be blamed on more than just the chemicals. It was difficult for Paul to communicate with Erin, and she was now four months pregnant.

Every time the two spoke to each other on the phone, it seemed as though it ended with a fight. Paul blamed the distance between them for the arguing. He missed Erin, and the alcohol and the pills was hardly a substitute. She was having his kid, and he had little to do with anything involving the pregnancy.

Paul picks up the bottle of vodka and downs it till it's completely finished. A soon as he throws the bottle away, he hears someone knocking at the door. Paul stands and walks to the door and opens it. "Yes?"

It's one of the crew members, a young guy named Diego. He tells Paul, "You're needed on the set."

"Okay, be there in just a second," Paul tells Diego, who closes the door and walks off. Paul walks to the mini-fridge, then grabs a bottle of water and makes his way out of the trailer and onto the set. It's actually a good little walk from the trailer to the set, so it takes him a few minutes.

Getting closer, Paul can now see trucks and equipment surrounding the building. He walks up and asks where he is needed, and one of the grips tells him they are looking for him upstairs.

"Fuck, are you serious?" Paul exclaims. "I got to walk all the way up there? Shit."

Paul makes his way through the building filled with extras and crew members running around doing all sorts of things. Finally, on top of the building, Paul sees Michael standing over to the side of the building, talking to Ben. Paul approaches them, glancing around at the surroundings and realizes they are filming the scene where Paul opened fire on the roof.

"Paul, come here." Michael pulls Paul over to join him and Ben. "Okay, we're trying to get this entire thing right so, we wanted to show you what we had in mind."

"Cool." Paul actually seems perky.

"All right, so Ben's you, and there's Anthony over there as Parker." Michael points over to the young actor, Anthony, who is portraying Parker in the film. "Okay, so can you play out to us what you remember on the roof?"

"Sure." Paul looks to the corner of the roof. "I was standing right over there, by the edge." Paul has everyone's attention while he speaks. "Parker would be about fifteen to twenty feet away, standing between me and the stairwell door. The door bust open, and we shouted for them to get down, and they opened fire. Then Parker spun like a top, and I shot the fuckers."

"Hey, Paul." Ben raises his hand and interjects." I thought Parker fired before you. I mean, I could be confused, but I thought that's what you said in the book."

"Fuck that stupid book. He changed everything."

Games Without Frontiers

Paul is not real sure where he's going with this. "They came up through the door and shot at us, hit Parker in the neck, then me in the foot, and then I killed them."

"Well, for creative-risk's sake and continuity, we will have Parker and Paul shoot," Michael interrupts. "They both get hit, then Paul delivers the final shots. Is that good, Paul?"

"Yeah, I mean, I just want it to be right."

Michael looks back to Ben. "So you got that?"

"Yeah, can I just ask you one question Paul?"

Ben turns his attention to Paul.

"Shoot." Paul smiles at Ben.

"So if you were right here, and Parker was right there, didn't he get in the way of the aim?"

"No, I dodged around him after he was shot."

"Paul, you just said that you two fired at the same time." Michael interjects as his own curiosity flares up a little.

"Look, Ben, you're a fucking actor. You have no fucking idea what it was like. I'm telling you what happened." Paul's entire demeanor changes with this comment, and he continues to plead his case. "He was there. I was here. They shot him. I killed them. End of story."

Michael walks and puts his arm around Paul. "Thank you so much, Paul. I think that's all we'll need for now. We'll call you if we need anything else okay, buddy?"

Paul doesn't say anything back. He makes his way back downstairs through the building. When he gets back to his trailer, he looks into the mini-fridge. He pulls out a bottle of whiskey, unscrews the top and begins swigging.

Some time goes by, then someone knocks on the door. Paul calls out, "Who the fuck is it?"

"It's Ben. Can I come in?"

"Yeah, it's open." Paul doesn't move at all. He sits in one of the chairs in the kitchen area of the trailer. Ben opens the door and walks inside. The entire trailer smells like a bar.

"Hey man. How are you doing?" Ben joins Paul in the kitchen.

"I'm fine. Fuck you care?"

"I haven't forgotten why I'm here." Ben stops for second, and then tells Paul." I didn't mean to, like, embarrass you, or anything like that. I mean, I owe my entire being here to you."

"Yeah, you do."

"Paul, I'm not trying to piss you off. I'm trying to be your friend."

"Yeah, I know, Ben. It's just everything they are saying about all of this is such fucking lies. I mean, it wasn't like this. They keep changing everything, and it's making me fucking crazy. I hate it." Paul almost looks as though he's about to cry, so Ben interjects.

"Paul, man, you're my friend; you helped me out more than anyone in my entire life, and I owe all this to you."

Games Without Frontiers

Ben wants to cheer Paul up, but really doesn't know how. "I want it to be real, just as much as you, but you know this is a movie. It's not real life. It's all fake."

"I've got other things on my mind other than just the movie. My girl is pregnant, and I can't be there 'cause I'm trying to do this shit."

"Damn, man, I didn't know that. Well, I mean, congratulations, you're going be a father."

"I want to be there so bad, but I'm stuck here."

"Well, Paul, in all fairness. I mean, this is all about you." Ben hopes this will help. "There wouldn't be any of this if it wasn't for you."

"Thanks, Ben. I needed that." Paul stands up." I appreciate you coming by; it's nice to know someone gives a shit."

"It's no problem." Ben stands up as well.

"You want to come and hang out for a little while tonight and not just sit here all alone?"

"Yeah, I would, but I'm going to try and get a hold of the wife. I'll take a rain check."

20.

June 10's

Filming was wrapped yesterday and Ben is back in L.A..
Tonight was going to be a huge wrap party. It was all very exciting.
Now that the filming was done, he was getting all kinds of offers on
other feature films, some of which included six-figure salaries. Ben
was going to start house hunting this week, take a few photo op's,
and speak with some of the exec's about the new parts he was being
offered. But tonight, he decided he would party like it was the end of
the world.

At the wrap party, which was being held on the top of the
Hilton Checkers, everyone was there having a blast. When Ben
arrives at the party, he's surprised that everyone is already there, so
he decides to make the fashionably late entrance.

Everyone is excited when he arrives. One real pretty blonde-
headed girl Ben has never seen before in his life walks up to him and
hands him a napkin with "Wanna Fuck?" written on it with her name
and number. Ben tucks the napkin safely away into his pocket.

Games Without Frontiers

One of the first people Ben runs into is Jerry, one of the film's producers, who runs up to him with a big high five yelling, "Wassup, man?"

"Hey, Jerry, what's happening." Ben exchanges high fives.

"Hey, kid, this is gonna be so big, yeah hoo." Jerry is obviously wasted off his ass. "Hey kid, we're gonna make so much fucking money. Hell fucking yeah!" Jerry is messing up his expensive suit with all this hopping around, which is very unusual for this tall quiet guy with a groovy haircut.

Ben's smiling and trying to calm Jerry down. "Shhh, shit man, calm down."

"Ha ha, fuck yeah, party!"

Ben grabs Jerry. "Calm down man." They both start laughing. Everyone at the party is a little lit, so it's all in good fun. Jerry wanders off, and Ben walks to the bar and has a drink. Lots of people come by to congratulate him, but it's not until he runs into Paul that things start cooking.

Ben is standing talking to a couple of the other actors at the party when all of the sudden Paul shows up.

Paul wanders up to the small group and interrupts their conversation. "Hey, wassup everybody." Everyone but Ben gives a fake small smile and seems to barely even acknowledge Paul.

"Hey Paul, this is great isn't it?" Ben smiles and turns to Paul. "What you been up to, buddy?"

"Oh you know, this and that." Paul seems anxious. "Hey, Ben, can I borrow you for a second?"

"Yeah, sure thing." Ben joins Paul off to the side of the party for them to talk in private.

Paul looks around nervously once before he starts speaking. "Hey man, I'm kinda in a tight spot right now. Can you loan me some money?"

"Well, yeah." Ben is a little surprised by the question. "How much do you need?"

"Ummm, well, how much you got?" Paul looks Ben dead in the eyes. For a moment Ben thinks he's kidding but then realizes he is serious.

"Paul ,what's going on?" Ben is concerned about his friend. "What do you need the money for?"

"Look, Ben, I can't get into all the details, but I need some cash quick!"

"Damn man, I think there's an ATM in the lobby. How much do want me to get?"

"Can you help me out with two grand? I promise I'll pay you back."

"Two thousand," Ben says aloud, and then quiets down some and repeats. "Two thousand?"

"Yeah, just this one time, I promise." Paul looks pretty desperate.

Games Without Frontiers

"I'll go get you the money." Ben wants to help his friend, and this seems like the only way he can do it.

"Thanks, man," Paul tells Ben. "You're saving me. I'll owe you."

Ben puts his drink down on a table and pulls out his wallet. "I'll run down there and meet you back up here, okay?"

"Up here is no good. I got a room in the hotel. Can you meet me there? it's fourteen-oh-eight. Is that okay?"

"Yeah, man. I'll go get your money and meet you up there. Don't worry about it, I gotcha." Ben exits the party and makes his way down to the ATM machine. He takes out the money, and then hops on the elevator up to Paul's room. When he gets to the room, the door is already cracked, so Ben knocks on it and it swings open a little.

Waiting to step inside, Ben first asks, "Hello?"

"Ben, come in." Paul's voice echoes throughout the room, so Ben casually enters the room. To Ben's surprise, there is young a guy in a really nice suit sitting in one of the guest chairs. "Ben, this is my friend, Pete." Paul is standing and walking around nervously.

"Hi." Ben extends his hand to shake. "Nice to meet you."

Pete stands and accepts the shake, very gentleman-like, and says," Hello, Ben, so you're the star everyone is talking about?"

Ben blushes a little. "Yeah, I guess."

"It's very nice to meet you, Ben."

"Our mutual friend here says that you can help us out with this little problem?" Pete in a very calm tone tells Ben.

"Ugh, yeah, I got the money. I suppose it's yours." Ben takes the wad of cash out of his pocket and hands it to Pete.

"Thank you." Pete takes the money, looks at it, but doesn't count it. He shoves it into his pocket. "It was very nice to meet you, Ben." Pete walks past Ben and stops for a brief moment next to Paul before exiting the room. "Look, you motherfucker, if you don't have the cash, you don't make the call. You're lucky. Normally, I don't have this kind of patience. I don't have time for this shit. Do you understand?"

"Yes," Paul says, looking down at the ground as if he were a small child that's just done something wrong. Pete exits the room and closes the door behind him.

"What was that all about?" Ben questions Paul with concern. "Are you in some kind of trouble?"

"Not anymore. My white knight shining through." Paul seems at ease now, so the tension in the room is no more. Paul walks to the bedside table and opens a small bag sitting on it. "You wanna go for a ride with me?"

"What the fuck are you talking about?" Ben smiles curiously and looks to see what Paul's doing.

Paul opens the little baggy and spreads out some white powder on the bedside table.

Games Without Frontiers

Paul leans down and starts to snort it. Ben a little surprised asks,"Oh shit, all this was over some fucking blow?"

"It's my other white knight. It gives me fucking wings, baby." Paul is rubbing some of the coke on his teeth the entire time he speaks.

"Jesus Christ, man, you need to get a handle on this shit if it's come to whatever just happened here." Ben walks over to Paul. "I mean, you want to get killed over this crap?"

"That guy's a pussy. He can't kill me, even he tried." Paul burst out laughing. "That's why I got this right here." Paul reaches underneath a pillow on the bed and pulls out a nine millimeter Beretta.

"Holy shit, where the fuck did you get that?" Ben's now a little uncomfortable as Paul pulls the gun out and waves it around a bit.

"I was in the Marines motherfucker. Where the fuck you think I got it?"

Paul laughs in genuine amazement. "Hey, look here." Paul spreads out a small line and hands a rolled up dollar bill to Ben. "Besides, it's your turn motherfucker."

Ben looks at Paul as if he can't be serious. "Look, I don't really fuck with drugs. That shit almost had me at one point in my life."

Paul doesn't like this response one bit. He points the gun at Ben. "It's your turn."

"Get the fuck out of here with that shit."

Ben pushes the gun away, and Paul just sits there laughing. "I don't need you pointing a gun at me. Fuck it, why not?" Ben bends down and takes a line. When he comes up his eyes are watering something fierce.

"Good shit, huh?" Paul smiles and laughs some more.

"Whew, fuck yeah. Damn, I can't believe you just talked me into that." Ben's actually a little happy he did the line now."So you got anything to drink?"

"Oh yeah!" Paul stands and walks to a suitcase and pulls out a bottle of whiskey and pours two glasses. Then he reaches into his pocket and puts some pills into each of the drinks. "This shit, will fuck you up." He hands the mixed drink to Ben.

Ben looks down at the drink, watching the little pill fizzing around. "What did you just put in this?" Ben notices that Paul's already finished his drink.

"Just little something-something that will put some hair on your chest." Paul smiles to let Ben know there is no reason to be afraid.

Ben lets out a small sigh and then downs the drink.

"Hell yeah!" Paul yells at the top of his lungs and then spreads out a couple more lines on the table. He hits one, then hands the dollar bill to Ben again to suggest that it is now his turn. Ben takes the bill, puts it to his nose and snorts another line, even though he really doesn't want it.

"What about the party? I can't go down there all fucked up."

Games Without Frontiers

Ben is still digesting the line of coke.

"Don't worry; we'll make our own party. We don't need those fuckers!"

"Well, okay, I guess." Ben actually kinda likes the idea of just hanging out with Paul. "But I want another one of those drinks."

"Fuck yeah." Paul grabs Ben's glass and pours them both another drink. This time the whiskey is filled to the rim and there are now two little floating pills in the drink. They both pound the drinks. "Hey let's go out and find some trouble!" Ben goes to stand up and feels a little light headed, so he sits right back down.

"Whoa, let's try that again." Ben stands up, this time walking around a little and stretching out. "So what do you have in mind?"

"There's a whole bunch of clubs around the corner. Let's go pick up some chicks."

"But aren't you married?"

"Not tonight, my friend. Not tonight." Paul is dead serious."Area codes, my friend. What she'll never know won't hurt her."

Ben smiles. "Are you sure?"

"Fuck yeah. Let's go out and find some bitches."

"We can bring them back up here." Paul points down at the floor while finishing the sentence. Then he walks into the bathroom, washes his face and squirts on a little cologne.

The two hit the streets, and while walking they come across a club called The Wall. On a flyer outside, it says they're having an eighties night. After seeing the sign, Paul suggests, "Hey let's go into that place."

Ben looks at the club then at the flyer. "Why do you want to go to an eighties night thing?"

"Because I was born in the eighties, thats why. So were you, right?"

"Yeah."

"So let's check it out." Paul heads toward the club entrance, and Ben follows right behind. They walk up to the bouncer, and the bouncer recognizes Paul and lets them in. Ben's not real sure how exactly Paul just got them in so quickly, but it's nice not to have to stand in line.

They walk into the club, and there's actually a pretty big crowd inside. Some people are dressed up in some whacky eighties clothing, most aren't. The music is blaring "Down in it" by Nine Inch Nails. Paul orders them both a screwdriver, and Ben shells out the money for the drinks and a tip. The two men find a nice little corner booth all to themselves. When they sit the music dies down a moment.

Ben checks out the inside of the club and is somewhat impressed. "This place isn't too bad." Ben's happy just chilling in the booth.

Games Without Frontiers

The club has a nice atmosphere, and it's going well with the buzz he's feeling. "You been here before?"

"Why?" Paul asks.

"The guy up front let you right in. He know you or something?"

"Nope, I just told him who I was, and he let me right in."

"Wow, man. That's pretty bad-ass."

"It pays off killing the world's biggest dickhead."

They both laugh. The music starts up again; it's really loud, so they quit talking to one another. While the two men sit enjoying their drinks listening to some Duran Duran song, a couple of girls across from the other side of the club seem to be making eyes at them.

"We should go talk to those girls," Ben leans in and yells into Paul's ear.

"Naw, wait just a minute. Let them come to us."

"Are you sure?"

"I guarantee, when they realize who I am, they'll want to fuck the shit out of me." Paul downs the rest of his drink and puts his arms behind his head. "Let them come to us. Trust me."

"Alright." Ben's shrugs and takes another slow steady sip of his beer. The beers cost ten bucks a piece and he doesn't want to have to buy too many – if any –more. Paul gets up to go to the bathroom, leaving Ben alone in the booth.

While he's away, the two girls approach the table.

One's blonde the others a red-head, both with white, silky skin and very pretty.

The blonde steps to the table and asks, "Hey, is that him, the 'Shot Heard Around the World' guy?"

"Yeah, that's Paul. I'm Ben. You ladies want to join us?"

The girls smile and slide up in the booth.

The blonde says, "I'm Holli. That's Melanie." The red head waves when Holli introduces her. "So your friend, he's the guy who …" She makes a gun out of her hand.

"Yep," Ben interrupts. "And we just got through making a movie about it."

"Really?" Both girls seem very interested.

"Yeah, that's how we're friends. I'm actually playing him in the movie."

Melanie smiles and says," Well, I guess we should get your autograph!"

"Sure, got a pen?" Ben laughs, and so do the two girls.

"Maybe later," Melanie says, making eyes at Ben, and he smiles back. The music starts up really loud once again, and as soon as the song is blaring, "Jeux sans frontiers." Paul comes back to the table with a really pissed-off look on his face.

"Ben, let's get the fuck out of here." Paul doesn't even acknowledge the two girls, who are staring at him.

"Why? I want you to meet my new friends."

Games Without Frontiers

Ben keeps a friendly tone and looks to the girls as if he is about to introduce them.

"Fuck these stupid bitches. Let's get the fuck out of here now." Paul turns and walks to the exit.

Ben stands, tells the girls he's sorry, and runs out the exit to catch up with Paul.

Paul is standing on the corner smoking a cigarette. Ben walks up to join him. "What the fuck, man, those girls wanted our nuts."

"I'm sorry, it's just that song." Paul keeps smoking. "I hate that song."

"Oh, so you want to give up on those hot babes because of a song?" Ben is confused.

"Listen, Ben, I'll tell you something I've never told anyone."

"Okay."

"When I was younger, there was this girl who had a thing for me, and she got all upset when I shot her down. Well, she ended up killing herself over something that I think was my fault."

"What?"

"She had a thing for me. I told her no, and she fucking killed herself. I don't know if it was intentional or an accident, but she's fucking dead. I've always blamed myself."

"Damn, but why the hatred for the song?"

"When I found out she was dead, the radio was on in my car, and that song started playing. I haven't heard it in years."

"'Games Without Frontiers'? No, me neither. I mean, I've always liked Peter Gabriel, but … shit, I had no idea."

"That song brings up some bad memories; I can't stand to hear it. Although, I still don't know what the 'she's so funky' part means."

"She's so funky part?"

"Yeah, the beginning, where he's likes, 'She so funky, yeah.'"

"He's not saying, 'She's so funky, yeah.'"

"I know, I know. That's just what it sounds like."

"He's saying, '*she sha frontier*.'"

"What the hell is that?"

"It's the name of the song. That's how you say it in French."

"How do you know that?"

"I just do. It's French. He's saying 'games without frontiers' in French, over and over again."

"Well, I can't fucking believe it. You have got to be shitting me?"

"Naw man, that's really it. Funny how things like that come back to bite you in the ass sometimes."

"What the fuck is that supposed to mean?" Paul seems a little angry now.

"I just mean, it's weird that … you know. Oh shit, I don't know …" Ben trails off.

"If you don't know, then shut the fuck up." Paul is obviously in a shit mood now, but he does manage to say.

Games Without Frontiers

"I'm sorry. I didn't mean that."

"So what do you wanna do?" Ben asks.

"I don't know. I guess we can go back to the hotel."

"Hey, I got this girls number earlier." Ben reaches deep into his pocket and pulls out the "Wanna Fuck?" napkin with the number. He shows the napkin to Paul.

"Holy shit, let's go back to my room and call her. Maybe she'll let us run a train."

"Ha ha, okay."

Ben follows Paul back to the hotel and up to his room. When their inside the room, they take down a couple more lines of cocaine and swig the whiskey. Paul still has the napkin, so he picks up the phone and dials the number. Ben's laughing the whole time.

"Um hello, is this Tracey?" Paul has the phone up to his ear. "Um, you gave me a napkin earlier ... uh, yeah, that's me ... Well, not much. What are you doing? Why don't you come on up to room one four zero eight ... Yeah, we'll be here— I mean, I'll be here ... Okay." Paul hangs up the phone and takes a big swig out of the whiskey bottle. "She's on her way up. She's staying here too."

"Oh no." Ben is laughing his ass off. "Please, don't do anything crazy."

"What me?" Paul pauses for a moment. "Never." They both laugh.

Paul sets the clock radio to a music station and turns it up.

"Hey, just don't put it on an eighties station. You know, just in case." Ben cracks up.

"Fuck you." Paul picks up a pillow and throws it at Ben, and then pulls out a pill bottle from the desk, opens it, pours a couple of pills into his hand and pops them. He hands a couple of pills to Ben and Ben acts like he's downing them, but decides to just stick them into his pocket. Around that time, someone knocks on the door. Paul stands, walks to the door, and let's Tracey in.

"Hi, I'm Ben's friend, Paul."

Tracey stops for a second and then sees Ben and decides to continue inside. "So, I thought you were up here by yourself. You didn't tell me you had any friends."

Paul speaks up. "Oh don't worry honey. I won't bite."

"Okay," Tracey says with a little hesitation in her voice. She turns her attention to Ben. "Hey."

Ben smiles and says, "Hey," back to her.

"You wanna drink?" Paul starts whipping up some drinks for everyone.

Tracey seems very uncomfortable, and this makes Ben a little uneasy. Paul doesn't seem to care in the least.

"No, thank you," Tracey answers very politely.

"'Kay then; your loss." Paul hands Ben a whiskey glass and keeps one for himself. "I got to take a piss. Be right back." He heads into the bathroom and shuts the door.

Games Without Frontiers

As soon as the bathroom door shuts, Tracey leans into Ben and whispers, "Hey, I don't want to be a bitch, but I'm not into whatever this is that you guys have in mind."

Ben starts feeling a little embarrassed. "I'm really sorry. Me and my friend were just messing around, and we found your number. I promise it was nothing. I feel kinda bad now."

"No." Tracey comes over close to Ben. "I just wanted be alone with you. Three's a crowd. I'm gonna get going, okay?" She kisses him lightly on the lips and turns to walk out of the room.

Paul stops her as he exits the bathroom. "Where are you going?" Paul puts his hand on her chest.

"I'm gonna take off." Tracey reaches to his hand and moves it away.

"Why?" Paul backs up to the door and stands in front of it so she can't go past him.

"Look, I got to get going. I just wanted to drop by. I gotta go." Tracey is starting to seem very impatient and not impressed much with Paul's position.

"Hey, Paul, she needs to go." Ben tries to back Tracey up, but his attempt is futile.

Paul doesn't budge an inch; he puts his arm around Tracey and tries to escort her away from the door.

"Look, asshole, I'm going. Get your fucking hands off me." Tracey tosses his arm away and tries to dodge past Paul.

"Stay right there, you fucking bitch." Paul grabs Tracey and throws her to the bed. "You're not going anywhere; this party is just getting started."Paul unzips his fly and pulls out his penis."Suck my dick, you fucking whore."

"What the fuck?" Tracey stands up and tries to fight a little. Ben tries to intervene.

"Paul, what the fuck. Let her go." Ben is trying to get Tracey free of Paul's grip.

Paul yells, "Listen, you two mother fuckers." He pulls out the gun he was showing off before from behind the pillow and points it at Tracey's head. "This bitch is gonna suck my fucking dick."

"Paul, put the fucking gun away," Ben tries to reason with Paul.

Paul points the gun at Ben. "You shut the fuck up." Then he points the gun at Tracey. "Suck it, you fucking whore."

Tracey is crying and her eyes are closed. She grabs Paul and starts going down on him. Paul keeps the gun to the back of her head but keeps looking directly at Ben.

Ben sits in shock, not really knowing what to do. He looks around to see if there's anything close by to hit Paul over the head with and maybe knock him out. But he has no such luck.

"Come on, man. Don't you want to fuck this bitch's ass?"

Paul points the gun at Ben and then at Tracey's behind. "What are you waiting for?"

Games Without Frontiers

"Naw man, I'm good." Ben sits in total disgust.

"You like that shit, don't you, you fucking pervert. You like watching this shit don't you?" Paul shouts out to Ben. "Just admit it, you want to be me, don't you?"

"No, not really."

"Why don't you just fucking leave then? You fucking pussy." Paul doesn't even seem to be paying any attention to the girl. He lets out a groan and comes in the girl's mouth. "Yeah, drink that shit, you fucking bitch." Paul grabs Tracey by the hair and throws her to the ground. "Get the fuck out of here."

She's crying heavily and runs out of the room.

"What the fuck, Paul. What are you thinking?" Ben is red in the face he is so pissed."She's gonna call the cops and tell them she just got raped."

"No, she's not." Paul seems very sure about this. "She's not gonna call shit."

"Man, I'm out of here. You're fucking crazy." Ben heads to the door, and Paul doesn't even try to stop him. "Dude, you need some fucking help."

"Do I?" Paul says in a very conniving way.

Ben slams the door as he exits the room. Exiting the hotel and walking down the street. Ben catches a cab.

"Where are you going?" the cab driver asks.

"Anywhere but here."

21.

August 10's

Paul was riding a bus back home to Erin, who was due any day now. A bus ticket was all he could afford, since he'd blown all his money. The last few months were nothing but a haze. He'd managed to stay completely fucked up until he was banned from everywhere that someone recognized him when he came around. The movie people took away his nice studio loft by the beach and canceled the credit card he had been issued. He couldn't charge up any more rooms now.

So he sits alone on the bus for the time being, trying to get a little rest. Nobody on the bus recognizes him, and that is just fine with Paul.

Going back home was now the only option Paul had, since he was broke, and no one would hire him for a military specialist job on any sets. Paul had unknowingly burned himself throughout the town, and his name was basically poison. No one returned his calls anymore. Paul had finally realized it was time to go home.

Games Without Frontiers

The bus ride is a long one. Luckily he had managed to score some coke for the ride home.

He was blasted more than ever these days; and on top of everything else, his foot was hurting really badly and the drugs weren't managing the pain well anymore.

After the long bus ride was over, Paul leaves the bus station on foot, walking to Erin's mother's house. Linda was letting Erin stay with her, and so now Paul was going to be joining the ladies. The last time he had spoken to Erin, he told her that there was really no reason for him to stay in Hollywood anymore and that he was taking the bus back. He made no mention that all the money was gone. Paul was more than welcome to stay at Linda's for the time being. This meant that he wouldn't have to pay rent, and that was a good thing because he was flat broke.

When he arrives at Linda's house, Erin waddles as quickly as possible to Paul. She's nine months pregnant now, making running not really an option.

"Hey, baby." Erin hugs Paul tightly as if to never let go. "I missed you so much."

"I missed you, too." Paul grabs her and hugs equally as tight.

"I'm so glad your back." Erin kisses Paul on the lips.

"So, your mom's cool with us being here?" Paul asks Erin.

"You know she loves you. She just wants us to have a place till you get on your feet around here. She can't wait to be a grandma."

"I can't wait to be a daddy." Paul smiles and kisses Erin on the head.

"Where are your bags?" Erin looks around Paul.

"I don't have any." Paul answers her question and tries to change the subject. "So, where are we gonna be put up?"

"I've been in the guest bedroom, which used to be my old room. I hope everything here is gonna be okay?"

"I'm sure everything's fine."

Erin and Paul enter Linda's house. Linda walks up to the couple and says, "There he is, Mr. Hollywood." Linda hugs Paul. "We're sure glad to have you back!"

"Glad to be back." Paul looks around for a moment. "The house looks nice. Can I use the bathroom?"

"You're home now; you don't have to ask," Linda explains.

Paul goes into the bathroom and closes the door behind him. He lays a line of coke out on the counter and snorts it, and then turns on the sink and flushes the toilet. Walking back to the living room, Paul overhears Linda and Erin talking.

"Why doesn't he have any of his things?"

"I don't know mom. I'm just glad he's back."

Paul waits a moment before making his presence known. He doesn't want them to know he could hear them speaking about him. Walking back into the living room, Paul tells Linda, "I really appreciate you putting us up like this."

"Oh, honey, it's no problem. I actually enjoy the company. It's nice." Linda manages to give a big smile.

"I guess I'm gonna start looking for a job tomorrow," Paul lets everyone know, including himself. "Hopefully I can find something close."

"Honey, if you need to borrow my car, I don't mind," Linda offers.

"Thank you, Linda." Paul accepts the offer.

"Honey, are you hungry? We've got some leftovers." Linda stands to walk into the kitchen. "I'll make you something. Hold on a sec." Even though he's not hungry, Paul smiles and nods.

Erin and Paul are alone in the living room now. Erin leans into to whisper. "What happened to all your things?"

"It's all gone." Paul shrugs.

"What do you mean it's all gone?"

"I mean that I have everything I own with me." Paul tries to smile, but can't. Much to his surprise, Erin doesn't seem mad at all.

"Just as long as your back." Erin hugs him very tightly.

Paul feels better about being there now; he thought she was going to kill him. But Erin doesn't seem upset at all – the eternal optimist. That was one of the reasons he loved her. This whole situation was going much better than he expected.

"I'm glad to be back here with you. I'm gonna find a job, then I'm gonna find us our own place, okay?"

"Okay baby." Erin kisses him and then says, "I think I'll have something to eat too." They stand up and to walk to the kitchen together, when Erin stops. "Oh, oh." She grabs Paul's hand and pulls it to her stomach. "He's kicking."

Paul feels the movement in her stomach. It surprises Paul how happy this makes him. For a moment, comfort washes over Paul's body as he realizes this situation isn't going to be as bad as he'd expected. Paul had been mentally ready for a blow-out between him and Erin, but it never happened, much to his surprise.

In the kitchen there are two plates of food that Linda has prepared for the couple. Erin sits and starts to dig in. Paul plays with his food a little and then struggles to swallow a piece of chicken. Swallowing it, he starts feeling sick, but manages to keep it down and not throw up. Sitting there together feels right, but Paul has no appetite whatsoever. He takes small bites and doesn't eat very quickly. Erin can tell that Paul is high as a kite, but says nothing about his strange behavior.

Linda asks from across the kitchen. "So, when's the movie coming out? I saw a preview and it looks good."

Paul looks up at her. "I really don't know. I'm officially out of the loop."

"Oh." Linda turns away and says nothing else about the movie.

Erin however mentions, "I saw they changed the title to *The Pain Cabinet*. I guess *Paul's Song* wasn't good enough."

Games Without Frontiers

"I really don't care anymore," Paul admits." I should have never talked to any of those people in the first place. They didn't even keep my name; they changed it to James. Who knows?"

"Well, at least you have a movie about you," Erin reassures Paul.

Linda wanders off to get ready for bed.

"Nobody knows who I am anymore. Nobody cares." Paul doesn't want to sound too depressing, but it's next to impossible.

"I care." Erin puts her arm around Paul's neck.

"I know." Paul looks to her and smiles.

"Well baby, it's late. I'm gonna get some sleep."

"Okay."

Paul kisses Erin goodnight. Linda has already gone to the master bedroom and locked the door, so he picks up the two plates and washes them. When they are washed off, he sticks them into the dishwasher. With no one around now, Paul walks over to the liquor shelves. He looks inside at the bottles. He sees an opened bottle of vodka, so he pulls out the bottle and pours a glass of straight vodka. Paul closes the cabinet door and leaves the bottle out. He walks outside to smoke a cigarette. Outside, he lights his cigarette and sits in one of the lawn chairs. The night is clear, and he can see all the stars. He isn't used to this. The pollution in the city made the stars impossible to see. Paul looks up at the sky for while, contemplating his options.

Hopefully, he would have some luck job hunting over the next few days. It was strange being back in a small town. He would have to adjust a little. It would take some time.

Paul falls asleep in the lawn chair.

22.

November, '10s

The room is hot and dark, and Ben is alone. The demon sits outside the bedroom door trying to find a way in. Ben can hear scratching against the wall. Ben's afraid that it will find another way in, but he's too afraid to move. The scratching against the walls is terrifying. He lies in the bed, afraid that if the demon finds a way to open the door, it will try to take his soul. This isn't the first time the demon has come. It breathes heavily and moves slowly. The door knob turns, and the door creeps open; there is nothing but darkness. Fear paralyzes Ben so much that it's hard to breathe.

Ben wakes covered in sweat, his breathing uncontrollable. He looks around the bedroom and calms down a bit. Ben wipes the sweat from his face – another bad dream. There's a girl in the bed next to him. She lies still and doesn't move. Ben slides out of the bed and tip toes to the bathroom. He turns on the sink and stares at himself for a second.

Ben leans down, takes a drink of water, and then splashes a little water onto his face.

Ben takes some deep breaths and walks back into the bedroom. He makes his way back to bed and gets underneath the covers, lying awake staring at the ceiling.

This was a re-occurring dream, and it was becoming more and more frequent. Every time, he seemed to wake up at the same point, never fully finishing the dream; but it always started the same way. Sleeping was becoming more and more difficult these days. There seem to be so much going on all the time that there was never enough time in the day for a good night's rest; and anytime it was more than just a few hours, it always seemed to end the same way.

Lying there, staring at the ceiling, Ben was mentally going over his schedule for the day in his head. Interviews, photos, promotions: they seemed like a never ending cycle. Trying to make himself just go to sleep was impossible no matter how hard he tried. *The Pain Cabinet* was in limited release and about to go wide over the next few weeks. With the early reviews in for the film, just about all of them were very positive, many were calling Ben the best new actor in town.

The movie seemed destined to be a huge box-office success; it was being promoted worldwide and receiving wild praise for its intense and accurate account of soldiers at war. The better the word of mouth was, as the news of the project spread, the bigger the movie seemed. It was destined to be an important film.

23.

November, '10s

Paul didn't enjoy his job much. He was working at a convenience store called simply Rest Stop. The days were long, and putting pressure on his foot while standing for long periods of time was making the pain consistently worse. Paul didn't have any insurance, so he could not afford to go to the doctor. The baby bills were stacking up as well. Erin and Paul were still living at Linda's house, so there were now four people staying in the two-bedroom house. They could barely afford basic necessities, even with Paul working all the time and Erin waitressing at night. Linda watched the baby while the two worked.

They named the kid Caleb, and they called him "Cal" for short.

The baby was still only a couple of months old and was quite simply the joy of Paul's life. He was working fifty to sixty hours a week, the pain swelling in his foot was getting worse and worse every day. Paul was drinking all the time to ease the pain – or that was his reasoning for drinking so much. He really couldn't afford to do anything but drink; he had no money for prescriptions and doctors. All he had to look forward to in his life was the bottle and Cal. The two managed to balance out all the bad.

The Rest Stop was slow and only paid Paul nine dollars an hour. It was one of the only jobs he could get. He had no education, and he was handicapped and broke with no skills. Being a veteran really didn't mean much. Most people who recognized Paul as the "Shot Heard Around the World" guy weren't as excited as they used to be. Most people had no idea who he was and mostly didn't care. Working at the Rest Stop allowed Paul a twenty percent discount on all items except gas, so he did all of their grocery shopping within the Rest Stop. Paul's job was just working as cashier, but every now and then he would wash the store windows or stock up a little on a few items. His primary purpose was standing at the register. He dealt with money, lottery tickets, tobacco, etc., and his job never really required him to leave the cash register alone.

The television was the only thing that kept Paul sane day in and out.

Games Without Frontiers

One thing that actually gave Paul a real sense of joy was during the commercial breaks of the show, sometimes a trailer for *The Pain Cabinet* would show every now and then.

This particular afternoon, Paul was doing his usual inventory on items, and it seemed as if there was a preview for *The Pain Cabinet* on during every break. There was going to be an interview with the film's star on a Hollywood access show. Paul hadn't even spoken a word to Ben since the night in the hotel, but he was actually looking forward to seeing the interview. The segment was on at a slow time during the afternoon at the store, so Paul was planning on watching the entire thing.

Paul was the only employee in the store at that time of day, so he could easily sneak off and get a drink from his alcohol-filled thermos. He filled it in the morning before work so that he would be able to have a few drinks throughout the day. Today, Paul had been having some major urges, so he was only half way through his work day and he was already pretty lit. It was nice being a little fucked up at work. It sure made the time go by faster. The entire day was slow, so Paul was enjoying his buzz immensely.

The interview was now on, and the only person besides Paul in the store was a young teenager who was probably shoplifting but Paul pays him no attention. He is too wrapped up with the television.

"Today our guest is the star of the new film *The Pain Cabinet*," Debbie, the host of the Hollywood Access show announces.

A clip of the film shows. Paul pays close attention to the scene, trying to figure out which part it would be in the story. There was his old pal, Ben, on the screen, sitting in a hummer, fully geared up. The camera shot is focused directly on him and no one else. He says, "You know, I don't know a lot, but I do know one thing." Ben pauses. "There are a lot of bad things out there, a lot a stuff I still can't look in the eye, but I can remember this one thing. If god is up there somewhere and he's looking at it too, how can he judge me for the actions a man takes? I don't know a lot, but I've already met my maker, and to tell you the truth, neither does he."

Paul had no fucking idea what part of the movie he had just watched. That conversation never happened, and he sure as hell didn't remember saying that. Paul's face turns red in anger. Luckily, he has his back turned to the costumer.

He opens up his little thermos and takes a very large swig. He pays close attention to the television. Ben is sitting on a stool across from Debbie. She introduces him to the audience and the crowd, mainly of women, go absolutely ape-shit. Ben smiles, waves out to the audience and blows a kiss, and you can actually hear a few girls having instant orgasms from his gesture.

"So, Ben, how are you feeling today?"

"I'm doing fantastic. How about you?"

Debbie smiles. "I'm great."

The two chatter on like a couple of schoolgirls.

Games Without Frontiers

Paul stares at Ben, who's constantly smiling and looks great. Paul feels bad for a moment for ruining their friendship and just wants to make amends.

"Um, sir?"

Paul turns around and the young boy is standing at the register. He's placed a package of Mentos and a diet coke two-liter by the register and stands there waiting to be checked out.

"Oh, hey. " Paul spins around with full attention to the kid. "Sorry, I was just watching this interview." Paul scans the items and tells the boy it will be three dollars even. The boy shuffles through his pocket for small change and places a bunch of quarters and a few dimes on the checkout table.

"That movie looks good," the kid tells Paul. "I wanna see it."

"Yeah, me too. You want to hear something funny?"

The kid smiles. "Sure."

"That movie is actually about me." Paul smiles proudly.

The kid looks at the television then back at Paul. "No way."

The kid doesn't believe Paul. "They just said his name was Sergeant James something. Your name tag says Paul." The kid laughs a little, and Paul doesn't say anything else. The kid leaves the store and Paul turns his attention back to the television and watches closely.

Debbie is talking about *The Pain Cabinet* and Ben's role as Sergeant James in the film.

She asks, "So I've heard that you went through some rigorous training to prepare for your part in the film?"

Ben smiles and answers, "Yeah, I spent Christmas in hell basically. It was all a little surreal. That training helped me so much for my mindset and focus for the role."

Paul laughs a little at how smug Ben is acting on the show.

"I had a lot of help on this picture. You know, I was kinda the new kid on the block the whole time."

A sense of jealousy creeps over Paul's mind while he stands there watching.

Debbie asks half jokingly, "So did they bully you around some?"

Ben answers her laughing. "Yeah, there were a few wet willies and a couple hurtz donuts along the way."

They both laugh. Debbie continues with questions. "I've heard that the real Sergeant James was on set and helped out with his input?"

Ben hesitates for a second. "Yeah, his real name is Paul, and he was a really great guy. He helped me so much, you know." Ben starts to say something else, but doesn't.

Debbie takes over the conversation. "Well the movie is *The Pain Cabinet*, and it will open everywhere this Friday. Don't miss it."

The interview ends and goes to commercial, and the commercial is actually a trailer of the film.

Games Without Frontiers

Paul continues to pay close attention to the commercial. Large words pop up between the scenes that say, "In a world where death is the only option, two soldiers made the ultimate sacrifice for freedom."

Paul chuckles a little at this and notices Patty, the night time girl, coming in the door.

"Hey, Patty." Paul waves and takes off his Rest Stop vest. "I got all the chips and drinks done today, so you'll just have to do the machines."

"Thanks, hun." Patty walks to the back and clocks in."You got anything to do before you get out of here?"

"There's some stuff in the back that needs to be put out, but not much." Paul walks to the back of the store and clocks out after Patty clocks in. "I'm gonna go ahead and get out of here."

As Paul walks by Patty, she stops and says, "Whew, you smell like a bar."

Paul turns and shrugs. "Sorry. I'll see ya later."

"Okay, hun."

"What did you just say?" Paul whips around quickly.

Patty looks up a little confused, "I said okay, hun."

"Oh, I thought you called me Ben."

Paul leaves out of the back of the store instead of the front. While walking out, he grabs a bag of some things he's gonna take home with him: chips, drinks, a couple packs of smokes.

Very carefully, he makes his way out without being seen with the bag. He walks down the street quickly, away from the Rest Stop, and once he is about a quarter of a mile away, he slows down.

Paul opens one of the packs of cigarettes, takes out a smoke and lights it.

Then Paul continues down the path home.

The path was about three miles and he didn't have the car today. He rarely got to use it. Erin was always taking it everywhere she needed to go. Paul didn't mind much. The walk gave him some time to think and have a little time alone even though it was hell on his foot. As soon as he got home, Paul was always busy with Caleb, getting him fed and getting him bathed. Lately, though, Linda was doing all this, so Paul didn't do much when he got home except drink. It didn't matter that his foot hurt every day; he felt the alcohol was the only thing that gave him any balance anymore.

About halfway home, Paul stops by the liquor store about a mile from the house. He walks to the back and grabs a large half gallon of cheap vodka and walks up front to check out.

The cashier recognizes him from daily visits. "How's it going man?" He takes the bottle and rings it up. "That will be eleven ninety."

"I'm all right." Paul hands the cashier eleven ones and nine dimes. "Here you go man."

"Thank you."

Games Without Frontiers

The cashier takes the money and Paul is out the door before he can blink. Outside he takes a small Dr. Pepper out of his little bag stash, opens it and pours about half of it out on the ground.

Paul opens the new bottle of vodka and pours it into the half-full Dr. Pepper. The Dr. Pepper bottle is now full again. Paul takes a swig of the vodka before twisting the lid on tight. Paul drinks the Dr. Pepper as if that was all it was. When Paul gets to his street, he's surprised to see Linda's car in the driveway. As he approaches the house, Erin walks out and hugs Paul.

Paul is a little uneasy and returns the hug. "What's wrong?"

"We talked about this, didn't we?" Erin is watery eyed, looking directly at Paul in the eyes."We talked about the drinking."

"Sweetie, I told you the only reason I drink is because my foot hurts so bad all the time; it's the only thing that takes away the pain."

"No, Paul, we talked about it three nights ago – this coming home drunk, passing out, and you told me you wouldn't come home that way again."

"What are you talking about?" Paul changes his entire attitude. "I drink because of my foot. Do you have any idea how much my fucking foot hurts me on a daily basis."

"I know, Paul." Erin's voice trails a bit, and she doesn't seem angry, just upset." I knew you weren't going to remember. I knew you were drunk."

"Remember what? I told you I was gonna lay off if it didn't hurt. Well, my foot fucking hurts, and I don't know what else to do." Paul's voice slurs a little and gets louder by the word.

"I don't either," Erin sighs. "Paul, we talked about this."

Paul interrupts. "We talked about what? What the fuck did we talk about? Is this all fucking riddles today?"

Tears start streaming down Erin's face. "I can't have you in mine and my son's life like this all the time. For god's sake, Paul, you passed out cold next to the crib the other night, and me and mom couldn't figure out whose vomit we were cleaning."

"Oh, I see, so Linda's kicking me out." Paul looks behind Erin to see if Linda is looking out a window from inside the house, which she is.

"This is fucking bullshit. I don't need this." When Paul turns around he notices that there are neighbors watching him now. "What the fuck are you assholes looking at? Mind your own fucking business."

The neighbors turn away and act like they aren't still paying attention, which they most certainly were.

"So I guess it's just Fuck Paul Day today."

"Look, Paul, you're not listening." Erin tries to calm Paul down some. She grabs his left hand and tries to hold it.

"Get the fuck off me." Paul jerks his hand away from her. "I don't need this shit right now."

Games Without Frontiers

"You won't even let me finish. I just want to ..." Erin is still trying to reason with Paul. He storms off anyways, fairly sure that the neighbors probably have called the police on him.

Paul walks down the road until he is close to a grocery store with some pay phones out front.

Paul stops at the pay phones and searches his pocket for a quarter. After searching his pants for a moment, Paul see's a a quarter laying on the ground next to the pay phone. He picks the coin up and inserts it into the pay phone. Paul realizes that the only number he knows by heart is Pete's, so he hangs up and grabs his quarter back. He decides to make his way out to the woods behind the store to try and find a place where he can sleep.

After walking around in the woods for a little while, Paul finds a small, covered spot underneath a tree. He spreads out to make the spot his own, then pulls out his bottle of vodka and begins quickly drinking it.

It starts getting dark outside and the animals are becoming very noisy.

Paul is pretty drunk now, so he lies down to try and get some sleep. He closes his eyes and curls up in the fetal position. After some time, he drifts off, the whole time thinking, *How did it come to this?*

24.

December 10"s

"I know, I know, that's great." Ben stands in the kitchen with his lab top schedule book in front of him and his house phone up to his ear. "Yeah, Thursday the tenth. Yeah, I got it."

Ben types into his schedule: "Lunch with the Coen's."

"Yeah, Liz, I got it. Thank you so much." Ben hangs up the house phone, picks up a glass of chardonnay that's almost finished and gulps down the drink. He then washes the glass out and puts the glass into the sink.

Ben walks through his dining room where there is a large standing mirror and looks at himself. He's wearing slacks and a nice button-down shirt tucked in – a very simple outfit that ran him about three hundred dollars. He looks nice.

Tom walks into the dining room. "Hey you ready to head out?" Tom asks. He also looks very nice with an almost identical outfit except for the colors.

"I was born ready."

Games Without Frontiers

Ben smiles doing one last once-over on himself. "You driving?"

"Sure." Tom smiles. "But hey, later on, we may be taking a cab."

"Fair enough." Ben walks behind Tom out the front door of the house.

Tom pushes a button on his keypad and his Lamborghini's engine fires up. It riles like a jet engine.

"I never get tired of that sound," Ben says and hops in the passenger seat. The night is only beginning. The two gentlemen have big plans, as there is a party at a really nice house that some big Hollywood producer owns, and they've both been invited.

When Ben's stardom starting hailing down, he made sure Tom had working parts in all of his new projects. Tom was becoming more and more successful in supporting roles, so he was able to take lots of jobs. The only parts being offered to Ben always seemed to be leading roles, so he was taking some time and being a little choosey with the consideration of his next roles. He wanted to do good work and wanted to be part of a project that would be something to be proud of.

Driving down the freeway and turning heads, Ben is feeling good, so he rolls down the window for fresh air. There is always great weather in California. Ben looks out over the freeway.

They pass by a couple of movie theaters where *The Pain Cabinet* is on the top of all the marquees. The success of the movie was already astounding. After grossing nearly one hundred million in less than three weeks, *The Pain Cabinet* was on the tip of everyone's tongue. Ben was picked to be the sexiest new star this year for Studio Weekly, and all this buzz was paying off nicely.

Ben looks and sees a billboard with *The Pain Cabinet* advertised on it. "Can you believe all this?"

"Believe all of what?" Tom keeps his eyes on the road, not sure to what Ben is referring.

"That it's happening," Ben smiles. "I mean, it's really happening, all the effort and hard work is finally paying off."

"Oh, yeah, we're lucky," Tom says, still keeping his eyes looking straight ahead. "So you know this place where we're going?"

"Yeah. I mean, I've never been there, but I heard it's really nice. It's like four square miles. It's fucking huge – belongs to some kind of producer."

"What has he done?"

"He's does those teenage shows, like the musical high school, then turns the kids on to record deals. Something like that."

"Oh, there will probably be some hot young girls there. Nice."

"I'd imagine, but make sure you check the birth date," Ben warns Tom. "Some of those girls look thirty years old and are barely sixteen, so be careful."

Games Without Frontiers

"So remind me," Tom interjects, "why are we going to some lame cradle-robbing party?"

"Lame?" Ben turns and looks straight at Tom with a shocked look on his face."You obviously don't know what you're talking about. There will be tons of pussy. I'm just saying make sure you don't end up pulling a Polanski." They both laugh.

"Right, so what are your thoughts on the comic book?" Tom says, changing the subject.

"I like the art. I mean, it's great ..." Ben's voice trails a little. "I just don't know if a superhero movie ... I mean, I just don't know."

"What don't you know? Aren't they offering fifteen mill' and two sequels?"

"If there are any sequels."

"Hey man, don't talk like that. It's *Qaudren Steel*; it's gonna be big."

"I just don't know. I just don't like something about a guy who walks around with a big electronic sledgehammer that sends out seismic waves when he hits something with it."

"You're gonna pass on that much money, because ...?"

"That's the only reason I'm even considering the part." Ben lights a cigarette without asking for permission first. "What do you have up next?"

"I just got the lead in a new Diaz romantic comedy, and I'm gonna take it. It's actually a clever little script."

"What's it called?"

"*Night and Dave*." Tom laughs a little as he says this.

"*Night and Dave* ... and my guess is you're Dave?"

"Yeah, it's a great role." Tom nods his head up and down. "I'd rather be Qaudren Steel though."

"No, you wouldn't. They said the costume suit weighs sixty-seven pounds."

"Holy shit." Tom's astonished."No wonder they're gonna pay so much."

Ben looks back out the window at another movie theatre playing *The Pain Cabinet*; this one has it on four screens. He smiles and throws the cigarette out the window, and then rolls the window up.

They arrive at the "party" and, driving up to the house.

Tom notices there are not really all that many cars parked outside. "Guess mom and dad dropped everyone off."

"Ha-ha." Ben looks around and sees that there are some really nice cars parked around the house hidden off to the side. "Hey look, they've got valet." A few young guys are dressed in nice little uniforms and are taking keys and parking the cars.

"Nice." Tom is impressed.

They pull up to the valet car guys and hop out of the car. One of the valets runs up to Tom and hands him a ticket. Tom gives him the keys and says, "Be careful."

Games Without Frontiers

The kid turns to Tom as he hops into the driver's seat, "Yes, sir." Then he hauls ass away.

"Shit." Tom watches his car fly off. "Hey, keep it under fifty, fucker; those cars are hard to find."

"Don't worry, nobody drives those anymore, I'm sure you'll find replacement parts somewhere," Ben says and pats Tom on the back. "Chill out, we're at a party."

Tom shrugs off the valet's driving abilities and turns to walk with Ben up to the party. There are some young attractive girls talking outside the front door to the mansion. Ben and Tom walk up them. "I heard there was a party going on somewhere around here."

The girls turn and toast their plastic cups. "Yep, get in here." The girls wave the guys inside.

Walking into the party, Tom and Ben look around, and Tom spots the bar. "Hey, let's go get a drink."

The place is packed. It's a huge fifteen-bedroom house, and there are two fully stocked bars, one inside and one outside.

Tom peeks outside. "There's no one at the outside bar. Let's go out there."

"Sure." Ben stands behind Tom. "Lead the way."

They walk outside where there is a huge swimming pool, with a giant rock waterfall; this area is less populated, so they walk straight up to the bar.

The bartender, a young sharply dressed guy, sees them heading his way, and when they are within speaking distance he asks, "Hey, wassup guys. Can I get you something?"

Tom smiles and says, "Can you make a Singapore Sling?"

"Yeah, sure. What about you, sir?" The bartender directs his attention to Ben.

"Can I get a shot of tequila, straight up, with a little salt on the rim; and what kind of beer you got?"

"Everything." The bartender looks around the bar a second and then looks back to Ben. "I mean, we don't have all the imports."

"How about a Beck's? Haven't had one of those in a while."

"Sure thing," The bartender hands Tom his drink, then pops the top of a Beck's and hands it to Ben. Then places a shot glass on the bar. "Any preference on the tequila?"

"Quervo's fine," Ben tells him.

The bartender salts the shot glass then fill's it from a quervo tequila bottle. Ben picks up the shot, drinks it quickly, and sets the empty glass on the bar. "Thank you."

"No problem, sir," the bartender tells Ben. "Saw the movie. It was great."

Ben nods his head and says, "Thank you."

Ben and Tom turn their attention to the pool and walk up to some lawn chairs no one is sitting at. They sit down by the pool.

Games Without Frontiers

The area is beautiful; there are palm trees everywhere, and the pool is blue like the ocean. The atmosphere is lit in interesting ways that make it just bright enough to see but still just dark enough. There's somewhere around fifty to hundred people outside at any given time, and almost everyone is in their early twenties. Ben and Tom chill with their drinks on their lawn chairs, all spread out and comfortable. There are a few girls in tight little bathing suits swimming around in the pool who attract most of Tom and Ben's attention.

"Nice party." Ben toasts drinks with Tom.

"It surely is that. My guess is the pool's heated." Tom brings his drink back down and takes a nice steady sip.

"Who cares?" remarks Ben.

They sit for a moment in silence and enjoy the scenery. A few moments later, a young blonde girl in a red dress walks over to Ben and Tom from inside of the party.

"Excuse me, but do I know you?" The girl is head-to-toe sexy. Her dress is tight, and she's tall with long legs and great curves.

Ben looks at her. "I don't know, do you?" He smiles flirtatiously. "I'm Ben, and this is my buddy Tom." Ben points to Tom, and he and the young lady exchange "hi's".

"You're in *The Pain Cabinet,* aren't you?" She blushes when she asks.

"Yep, that's me." Ben is very confident in his tone.

"I didn't catch your name."

"Oh, I'm sorry." She puts her hands to her side. "I'm Beth. It's just it's so nice to meet you. I'm sorry I'm a little nervous."

"Don't be nervous." Ben pulls his feet up, so Beth can sit on the edge of the fold-out lawn chair. "Have a seat."

"Okay." Beth sits. Now that she is much closer, Ben can see that she is flawless. Her face is smooth, her lips dark red, and she has beautiful green eyes that seem to sparkle when she speaks. She has an amazing body, and is very sexy with her mannerisms.

Ben smiles and asks, "So how did you wind up at this party, Beth?"

"Oh, I'm playing a supporting part on *The Family Tree*. It's a new show. They're gonna do a six-show run, see how it does." Beth crosses her fingers. "So, hopefully …"

Tom looks over. "Hey, I actually got offered a part on that."

Beth smiles. "Really? Which part?"

"I honestly can't remember, but the show was cute," Tom says, trying to not let on that he thought the show was poison.

"A bunch of the cast is here." Beth looks around. "Somewhere." She looks back at Ben and shrugs.

Tom looks over and notices that Beth is now placing her hand on Ben's knee. Trying his best not to be a buzz kill, he asks, "So Beth, how long you been an actress?"

"Oh, all my life."

Games Without Frontiers

Beth doesn't even acknowledge Tom; she just keeps looking right at Ben.

Ben can tell what Tom's getting at, so he follows up with, "And how long is that?"

"Nineteen years," she smiles.

Neither Ben nor Tom can tell if she's lying.

"So I was wondering are you guys gonna hang out here for a while?"

"Why?" Ben asks.

"Well there's another party going on tonight, and well it's ..." She blushes a bit. "I don't know, a little hotter." She leans and kisses Ben's neck. "You wanna come?"

"I just did," Tom adds to the moment.

Beth leans back to eye level with Ben,."You can bring your friend if you want?"

Ben looks over to Tom. "Hey Tom, you wanna go to a party with Beth here?"

"I'm game." Tom stands up without hesitation. "I'll go get the car."

Tom leaves the two sitting by the pool.

"Where is this party?" Ben asks.

"In the hills. I've got directions on my phone," Beth tells Ben. "It's in my purse. I'll go get it."

"We'll meet you outside."

They both stand up and walk off in opposite directions. Ben walks back out to the front of the house.

Tom has just hopped into the car.

Seeing Tom, Ben walks over to the passenger side and opens the door. "Hey, she's on her way; she had to get her purse."

Tom nods his head and starts playing with his IPod that's connected to the stereo in the car. Tom plays "Fight For Your Right" by the Beastie Boys and turns up the volume.

Beth walks out front. Tom and Ben both wave to her, and she walks up to the car.

"You'll have to sit in my lap," Ben tells Beth as she gets in the car.

"Okay." She smiles and gets in.

They start out of the driveway, and Beth tells Tom the directions to the new party. "We'll have to stop before we get there."

"Why?" Ben and Tom say at the same time.

"All right, guys, this may sound weird, but everyone there will be wearing masks."

"Masks?" Tom remarks with confusion. "What do you mean?"

"This party, its real exclusive. Everyone there will have Mardi Gras masks on. It's part of the fun of the whole thing, not knowing who the other people are."

"Sounds kinky." Ben is intrigued by this, and Tom is a little weary.

Games Without Frontiers

"So, do you have to wear a mask?" Tom asks.

"I don't think they'll let you in without one, so yes."

"We need to stop and get some masks then." Ben is always ready for anything. "Let's just stop at a party store and get some cheap masks."

"I've already got mine." Beth reaches into her purse and pulls out a small masquerade ball mask made out of ceramic and puts it up to her face.

"You like?"

The face of the mask looks like a woman with no particular expression on her face, and there are multi-colored feathers coming out of the top of the mask.

"It's flamboyant; I like," Ben says and smiles. "Let's go get some masks. Get off at this exit. There's a costume shop down that way a little."

They find the costume shop and Ben runs inside and buys a couple of masquerade ceramic masks, both somewhat masculine looking. He hops back into the car and pulls the masks out of a bag. "Which one do you want?"

Tom looks at the masks. They're both basically the same. He points at the one with blue feathering. The other has orange feathering on the top.

Ben puts the mask on. "How do I look?"

Tom gives Ben a thumbs up, and Beth says, "Good enough to eat." She has an incredible smile. Too bad she's gonna hide it under a mask.

Ben doesn't say anything, but the thought of this party was making him nervous; he really has no idea what to expect.

Tom has some rap music playing in the car. Beth turns the volume up. "Hell yeah!" She's bouncing all over Ben's lap, which is turning him on big time. Her ass and breast are rubbing against him, and he can barely contain himself.

They get to the party, which is way off in the hills, somewhere Tom and Ben didn't even know was there. Its dark out now, and there are no streetlights, so it's almost pitch black. The headlights of the car are the only guiding force, and the GPS isn't even registering.

When Tom pulls the car up, he parks next to some other nice cars and a few limos. There's no one standing outside. When they exit the car together, Beth says, "We need to put on the masks before we go inside, or they won't let us in."

The three of them each slide on their mask and walk to the front. When they get to the mansion's front door, two men are standing in front of it, both dressed in tuxedos and both with unusual animal masks on.

As the trio walks to the front, one of the men puts his hand in the air and asks, "Goodvevening, may I have the password please?"

Games Without Frontiers

Beth takes over. "Fidelio," she tells the men.

"Thank you," the man tells her, and the two men open the front doors and let the trio inside.

As they walk through the front door and into the hallway, there is only another man wearing a tux and a mask, standing in the hallway. He lifts his arm to welcome them and points them in the right direction.

Walking from one room to the next in the large house, Ben sees people all over the place. Some are naked and having sex right in front of everyone, some people stand around watching, some not paying any attention at all and just chatting away. There are cameras on tripods and televisions relaying the images in the corners of the large rooms. Ben looks and notices that Tom and Beth are no longer walking next to him. He has no idea where they have wandered off too, so he tours through the house a little more. A girl with a beautiful body, wearing nothing but a mask, walks up to Ben.

The girl extends her hand and says, "Hello."

Ben turns to the naked girl and says, "Hi."

"Are you new to this?" she asks him.

"Yes, I am," Ben says, being honest.

"Come with me. I'll show you around." She turns and starts walking through the house. Ben follows closely behind. "Down here is for people who watch and like to be watched," she tells Ben as they walk through this rather large orgy to the next part of the house.

She points to a section of the house as they walk by. "If you go down there, it's for girls and toys."

Ben turns and can see through a doorway into one of the rooms. There are two girls with a strap-on having sex, and some guys are jacking off. Another naked girl with a small paddle walks up to the girls and starts spanking her.

"Holy shit." Ben is totally wide-eyed through the mask. He continues following the girl as they walk next to a staircase.

She points upstairs. "Up there is groups and couples who swing," she tells Ben as they walk by. There are two guys running a train on a girl right on the staircase. "Follow me back here." She grabs Ben's hand and leads him off. They walk into a rather small room where there are two girls lying on a bed touching each other passionately. One has a candle and is pouring the wax on the other, who is moaning in pleasure. The girl turns to Ben. "You're going to be our play toy," she says and pushes Ben to the bed.

The two girls lying there turn their attention away from one another and focus on Ben. They unbutton his shirt and take it off. They rub their hands on his chest and their tits on his back.

"You're ours now," the girls tell Ben.

The one who showed him around grabs his pants and tosses them off. They fight over his underwear, and Ben is still a little shocked at his surroundings. For a second he thinks this can't possibly be safe, then Ben says, "Fuck it, why not?"

25.

January 10's

Paul starts the day off vomiting into the toilet. He is in the bathroom of his one-bedroom efficiency apartment, and he's just woken up and is sick to his stomach. This has become a daily routine. Paul was drinking almost constantly these days. Somehow, he was able to function enough not to lose his job, so his life basically consisted of working and drinking. Paul didn't see very much of Erin and Cal. She wanted full custody and had hired a lawyer. Paul couldn't afford a lawyer, so Erin was getting everything she wanted. It was surprising to Paul how quickly she had turned on him.

Paul finishes and washes his mouth out in the sink. He walks to an open bottle of vodka and takes a big swig. "Ah," he lets out after the drink. He takes a thermos out of the sink, washes it, then fills it to the rim with vodka.

He dresses in his work clothes and turns on the television – the only other thing in the apartment aside from the bed. The news is on: "Man shot down by police after a daring raid."

Paul doesn't pay much attention. Same old shit, different day. Nothing was ever about him anymore, which always disappointed Paul. How quickly that all passed.

Paul sees the time on the news channel and decides he better head off to work. He leaves out the door and, on his way, drops by the mailbox and opens his box with a key. There are a couple of bills and a strange letter. He doesn't recognize the sender's address.

Paul doesn't open it yet. He closes the mailbox, and hears someone call out his name from behind him. Maybe a fan? Paul turns with a smile on his face.

A thirty-something guy in a nice suit is walking towards Paul. The guy smiles and asks, "Are you Paul?"

"Yes." Paul extends his hand to shake, but instead he receives a hand full of papers. He looks down in confusion.

"You've just been served." The young man turns and walks away.

Paul is speechless. He didn't expect this at all. Looking through the divorce papers, it all sets in for real. Paul tears up some but is careful to wipe it quickly so no one can see him crying. Paul takes the papers and puts them into a stack with his mail, and then he turns his attention back to the letter with the unknown sender. Paul opens the envelope. Inside is an invitation to a celebrity golf match. Paul is extremely surprised as he reads on further; it's a charity event, to which he has been cordially invited. He smiles.

Games Without Frontiers

There is a number to call and R.S.V.P. for the event, which he plans on calling as soon as he gets to work. The match wasn't until May; there was no way he was missing it. Paul only lived about a mile from the Rest Stop, so it didn't take that long to walk.

Paul's not worried about the court papers at all. He's so excited to be invited to the golf tournament. Paul gets to work about ten minutes late and is surprised that the owner "Kent" is there. Paul says, "Hey Kent, what's up?"

"Carla called in sick, and I didn't have anyone else. I knew you didn't have a phone so ..." Kent doesn't seem very happy. "Since you're here now, I'm heading out."

"Okay." Paul clocks in and turns, seeing that Kent is already out the door. Paul walks over behind the counter and changes the television station till it's on some cop show that shows police standoffs and shootings. He looks around and finds a clipboard with the morning inventory sheets still not filled out, so he fills them in himself, looking and guessing instead of actually counting anything.

A couple of people come in and out, buying gas and a few other things. Paul is able to follow the show since he's not that busy. There's a car chase from a helicopter's point of view on the show. This guy being chased is in a nineties Honda civic, running to an excess of a hundred miles an hour and being tailed closely by about a dozen police cars. It eventually turns to a standoff when the civic runs out of fuel.

The guy gets out of the car and fires at the cops. They take him down.

A young guy walks into the store and up to the counter to buy a pack of gum. Paul still watches the TV. While he rings the guy up, the young guy interjects. "Awww, shit man, I remember that one." He's obviously referring to the car chase. "Yeah, that fucker gets shot down. They unload on his ass. Watch ..." The guy points at the television.

Paul rings up the gum and tells the guy the total. "It's a dollar, seven. Yeah, I love these cop shows. I don't think I've seen this one."

The guy hands him a five and Paul makes change.

The young guy takes his change."Yeah, if you got to go out, that's how you do it, I guess." He exits the store.

A commercial comes on. "See the film that made over a hundred ten-best lists, now nominated for eight golden globes including Best Picture and Best Actor." It's a commercial for *The Pain Cabinet*. Paul turns all his attention to the television; it still makes him smile to see anything mentioned about the movie.

Some time goes by, business as usual at the Rest Stop. Paul goes to the back about halfway through his shift and turns off the camera that points directly at the counter. That way he can drink comfortably with no judging eyes upon him.

It's almost midnight; Paul is about halfway done with his shift.

Games Without Frontiers

He's counting the packs of cigarettes behind him and is listening to the TV. It's some sitcom that Paul's not really paying a lot of attention to. Paul is feeling kind of buzzed, and since no one's inside the store at this moment, he picks up the phone and calls the number on the golf invitation. Paul leaves a message that he will be there, and then hangs up the phone.

About thirty-seconds goes by and he picks up the phone again. He dials Erin's number. Two young men wander into the store as Paul makes this call. Paul doesn't pay much attention to the young men. He gets Erin's voice message and leaves a message. "Hey, it's Paul, I got served papers today." He pauses and takes a deep breath. "Look, all I want is to be in my son's life. I know you don't want anything to do with me."

The two young men come up to the front counter. They each have hoods on, and Paul can barely see their faces.

"I'll talk to you later." He hangs up the phone and turns his attention to the young men. "Can I help you guys?"

"Yeah." One steps to the counter and the other walks to the door and looks outside. The one at the counter reaches into his pants and pulls out a hand gun. "Motherfucker, open up that fucking register," he says, pointing the gun at Paul's face.

Paul stands unsteadily in shock and raises his hands.

"Okay, man." Paul slowly reaches to the register and opens it up. "There you go. Just take it."

"I will, motherfucker." The young thug hits Paul over the head with the butt of his gun. Paul drops to the ground, and the young thug jumps over the counter and starts unloading the cash into a plastic bag, "Stay down, or I'll fucking kill you." One of his hands grabs cash out of the drawer; the other holds the gun to Paul's head.

Paul sits silent for a second, dripping in the blood running from his head. It doesn't hurt as bad as it should. He looks up at the robber. "Do it, you fucking pussy."

"What did you say, motherfucker?" yells the gun man, looking down at Paul. "Don't think I won't kill you." He cocks the gun and presses the muzzle to the temple of Paul's head.

"No, you won't. You don't have it in you." Paul looks directly into the thug's eyes.

"Man, forget about him. Let's get the fuck out of here," the other thug is yelling at the top of his lungs.

"You don't have the fucking balls, pussy." Paul spits at the thug, barely hitting his legs.

"Fuck you." The robber hops back over the counter, and they both run out of the door. Paul takes some deep breaths and stands up after a few minutes. Then he dials 911.

"You reached the emergency line. What's your emergency?" a lady's voice on the police band.

"Yeah, I'm Paul. I'm in the Rest Stop, right off the highway. I've just been robbed."

Games Without Frontiers

Paul picks up the phone and carries it with him while he walks over to the ice and pulls a bag out and breaks it up.

"An officer is on the way. Please stay on the line." The operator keeps Paul on the line, asking questions until an officer gets there.

It doesn't take very long. An officer shows up, gun in hand. "Are you all right, sir?" The officer rushes over to Paul. He starts talking into his dispatch radio. "We need emergency medical unit. Sir, I've got an ambulance coming. Are you all right?"

"Yeah, I think so." Paul stands with ice to his head still. He's managed to stop the blood by wrapping a towel around his head.

"Sir, why don't you have a seat right here." The police officer grabs Paul and helps him sit on some stacked cases of beer. The officer takes over the situation. Other officers arrive, and so does an ambulance. The medics take Paul to the back of the ambulance and look at his head. He tells them he has no money to go to the hospital. They try to change his mind but are unsuccessful.

Paul sits on the back of the ambulance while the medic patches up his head a little.

Kent shows up as well. He parks his car and runs over to the ambulance to see if Paul is okay.

"Paul, man, how are you feeling? Are you okay?" Kent asks.

"Not so good." Paul sits in extreme pain. "They hit me over the head."

"Don't you worry man." Kent pats Paul on the shoulder. "You did good. I'm going to go inside and check the tape, then we're gonna get these motherfuckers." Kent walks off.

Paul gets sick to his stomach. The thought of what Kent was going to do to him when he gets inside and sees the camera to the counter is unplugged made him sick.

26.

April 10's

The Pain Cabinet won three Oscars, including Best Picture. The hype throughout the months was unbelievable. Offers were coming from everywhere. Now that the awards season was over, Ben was on the set of a thriller called *Syphon Graph.* At the last minute, someone had dropped out of the part of Kal, which was only a supporting character that Ben took the part of before filming. It was a typecast role considering the character was an ex-soldier who worked as a freelance mercenary. This part, however, was a much more fun role. Kal shows up in the last half of the film and basically does nothing but kill people and blow shit up. It required only two weeks of filming for his character, so this was a nice chance to do some work while deciding his next role. Plus, for the two weeks Ben was there, he would be paid seven million dollars.

Ben was filming a scene today where his character was in the background with very few lines. He had his lines memorized in no time at all.

So while they were setting up the scenes, Ben hung around with some of the other actors on set. Standing behind Ben in this scene was a girl character called "Sonja," who was a bad guy in the movie. The actress portraying "Sonja" had caught his attention.

Sonja was played by Krista, who was nothing more than a pretty face whose only work was some late-night cinema shows. Krista was super hot and Ben couldn't help but check her out. She was also a very sweet girl. She smiled a lot and was kind of goofy with her sense of humor.

They were hitting it off nicely, which was making the experience highly enjoyable for Ben. When Ben introduced himself to her earlier in the day, she smiled and told him she thought he got robbed of an Oscar nomination, and that it was a pleasure meeting him. Hours after meeting one another, they were still talking and joking about the movie business. Ben was so nervous thinking about asking her if she wanted to hang out with him that night after filming, he was shaking. He shouldn't have been though. She asked him before he even got the chance to ask her.

After they wrap shooting for the day, Krista and Ben stop around the corner from the studio at a Starbucks. Krista tells Ben how much she loves latte's and says he should try one, so they both have one. Ben tells Krista why he moved to California and how lucky he was to be where he was at this moment. They had this in common; she had also had struggles of her own getting here.

Games Without Frontiers

She came from a rich family that basically disowned her when she told them she wanted to be a singer and an actress. Krista had left home when she was eighteen and never looked back.

She'd been in California for a few years now. After being made fun of by Simon in an *American Idol* audition, she had decided to only persue her acting career. The best jobs she'd gotten so far was a guest spot on a television show and some bit parts in some really inexpensive straight-to-DVD movies.

Krista met a producer at a strip bar she was working at and had landed this part on *Syphon Graph*. Krista said nothing else about how she got the part.

Krista was a bubbly little thing. She was about five foot seven with a great body. Her outfit was this tight, black leotard-looking dress, which she filled out very nicely. She was only skin and bones except for her boobs, which she kept trying to convince everyone were real, but it was obvious they weren't. Krista had brown curly hair and brown eyes that matched. She had a smile taped to her face all the time. Ben had never seen someone who smiled so much.

They had both had fought to get where they were and – even though Ben had gotten further – their stories were similar. At one point during the conversation, Ben asks Krista, "So are you seeing anyone?"

Krista blushes and smiles. "I'm not really looking for anything, but I'm not seeing anyone, no." Krista has Ben's full attention.

"You know, I just feel kinda like a free spirit. I just don't like to settle."

"Kinda a little crazy, too?" Ben smiles and asks smoothly.

"Maybe." Krista smiles back flirtatiously. "So, Ben, how about you?"

"So how about what?" Ben knows what she's asking but wants to hear her say it.

"You have a special girl, or a special guy?" Krista asks, making fun.

"Yeah, his name's Roman." Ben puts his arms in the air. "He sings to me at night, so I can sleep."

"Sounds healthy." Krista plays along.

"I never have to worry. He's always got my back, literally."

They both laugh.

Ben continues, "No I'm not seeing anyone."

"That's a little hard to believe," Krista says. "I thought you were the flavor of the week."

"Just haven't, you know, met the right person." Ben blushes. "I've actually been really busy. It's kinda hard to juggle in a relationship."

Krista smirks at Ben.

He asks her, "Has anyone ever told you that you have an amazing smile?"

Her smile gets a little bigger and she rolls her eyes.

Games Without Frontiers

"Yeah right." Krista looks away. "So, Ben, what do you do when you're not working?"

Ben sits for a moment then starts to answer. "Well , honestly, I've been working nonstop for the past year. I was barely getting by before *The Pain Cabinet* role came along. I never really got to get out much. I was taking any job on just about everything I could find, just to make rent, which sucked because I got evicted from my place."

"Really?" Krista smiles and tilts her head in fascination.

"Yeah, I was actually sleeping on my buddy Tom's couch, but ever since then it seems my life is even busier." Ben looks out the front window of the coffee shop and notices that it's getting dark outside. "So what should we do, it's getting to be night now."

"I don't know." Krista shrugs off the question. "What do you have in mind?"

"You want to go get some dinner?"

"I'm really not that hungry. I'm in the mood to play some arcade games."

"There's this bad-ass place called Super Fun Castle around the corner a little ways. They have all the classics like Galaga and Space Invaders."

"God, I haven't played an arcade game since I was a kid," Ben admits.

"It's the only way to play games. Fuck the loser box and the PS." Krista laughs.

"You might get hurt if you say that too loud." Ben looks around at the nerdy people inside the Buckies, which happens to be everyone. "We should probably get out of here."

Krista laughs. "Yeah, okay."

They leave together and walk down the street towards the arcade. They're in Hollywood and it's getting late, so walking down the street probably means running into some paparazzi. Ben and Krista try to sneak around the streets so as not to be seen or hassled by photographers. They are successful until they are about a block away from their destination, when one lonely photographer spots them. The guy grabs his camera as Ben and Krista speed up their pace to the Super Fun Castle.

The videographer has his camera pointed right on the couple and asks, "Hey, Ben, how's it going?"

Ben's on camera whether he likes it or not at this point. He knows this video will be seen probably on television and the internet. Ben acts cool as usual. "Just hanging out. Gonna play some video games."

Krista laughs at Ben's response.

"Is this your new girlfriend?" the camera guy asks.

"This is my co-star and friend on *Syphon Graph*, Krista." Ben introduces Krista to the cameras.

Games Without Frontiers

He can tell she enjoys the attention, because she's slowed down considerably now that the camera guy was speaking to them. She's all smiles, and so is Ben until they reach their destination.

Walking inside, Ben tells the camera man, "All right, take it easy, man." They enter the Arcade and the paparazzi guy doesn't follow. He turns and walks back into the street.

Walking into the Super Fun Castle, Krista looks over to Ben and asks, "That happen to you much?"

He answers, "Ever since the movie, yeah kinda."

"Wow, that must be pretty cool." Krista seems a little jealous of the attention Ben was getting, but Ben shrugs it off.

As they walk around inside, Ben sees the place isn't a joke; they have everything.

"God, it's been for ever since I've seen Sunset Riders." It's one of the first games Ben notices. "I used to play that game when I was a kid." Ben then nearly faints as he turns to see the Teenage Mutant Ninja Turtles arcade game. "I probably spent about a thousand bucks on that game when I was a kid."

"Let's play." Krista walks over to the quarter machine and pulls a five dollar bill out of the pocket of her tight jeans. She grabs the large handful of quarters and walks back over to Ben."So who do you wanna be?"

"You know, I could have got that," Ben lets Krista know. He doesn't want her to think he is cheap.

"I'm the one who wanted to come here, so don't worry about it."

Krista says, always smiling." I want to be Leonardo."

"That's cool. I'm always Michelangelo." They both insert quarters on their character's spots and the game begins. Ben is surprised at how good Krista is at the game, and how bad he has gotten at it over the years. "Crap, I suck."

Ben's uses up all his lives and deposits some more quarters, while Krista continues to pound away at the bad guys without any of Leonardo's health depleted. Ben tries to play a little better, but he is no match for her; she's awesome. She keeps bumping into him with her butt while bouncing around, and Ben doesn't mind much. Krista seems to be really getting into the game. She starts yelling and jumping around after she beats one of the levels bosses. When she starts hopping around, every guy in the place turns and looks.

Ben depletes the last of the money and dies for a last time. Krista keeps going strong for a few more minutes, until alas, finally she dies.

"Awww, that's bullshit," Krista tells the game, and then turns to Ben. "I'm pretty bad-ass, aren't I?"

"You have no idea." Ben puts his arm around her and leads the two of them off. "I think you just became the woman of every guy's dreams in this place." She smiles and looks around noticing all the guys were trying not to stare at her.

Games Without Frontiers

"I'll have to let them know that I'm not available." Krista turns her attention back to Ben.

"How are you going to do that?" Ben asks.

And then without any warning she grabs the back of Ben's neck and closes in for a kiss. It's a soft gentle kiss, one that feels so good Ben almost feels weak at his knees. They kiss for a good minute or two. Ben puts his arms around Krista.

She leans back and looks at Ben in the eyes. "You think that will convince them?"

Ben smiles oblivious to his surroundings. "Yeah, I think they got the idea." Ben almost forgets where they are for a second. "Krista I think you just become my favorite person to be around."

"That's funny," Krista tells Ben. "I was thinking the exact same thing."

27.

April 10's

Since the robbery, Paul was only scheduled one day a week on the Rest Stop's work calendar. Kent wanted to get rid of Paul, and this was his way of doing it. Coincidently, Paul got some money in the mail recently from his small percent of the take on his book and movie.

The check wasn't huge, but it was still nice and gave him a little leverage for living expenses. Anything was better than nothing, even though in Paul's mind the check should have been for a lot more.

At a bar that Paul was beginning to frequent, he met a fan, Buck, who told Paul he could get him a job on his used car lot. So Paul wasn't going to show up for shifts at the Rest Stop anymore and would live off this little stash of money between transitioning jobs.

Games Without Frontiers

Tonight, Paul is having a drink at The Rusty Nail Saloon. He was a regular and knew everyone that worked at The Rusty Nail. Paul is contemplating what to do with the rest of the night. He is beginning to feel buzzed, and there isn't anyone else at the bar tonight and nothing on television.

Since the place is pretty much dead, Paul sips his drink while playing darts keeping himself amused.

The bartender, Jeb, washes out some empty glasses and then wipes them with a towel. He hollers to Paul across the place, "Hey, hero, you ready for another one?"

Paul looks at his half-full glass and yells back, "Yeah, I'll take another." Paul throws at dart and hits a bull's-eye, then walks over to the bar to finish his current drink. Paul places his empty glass on the bar, and Jeb exchanges it for another fresh one. Paul looks around the bar to check and see who's showed up while he's played a game of darts. Only a couple of small groups of people chattering amongst themselves – and one of the regulars, an older guy named Ron – are inside the place.

"What's going on, Ron?" Paul turns his attention to the other regular.

"Anything new in the dry-cleaning business?" Ron owned a couple of dry cleaners that pretty much ran themselves.

"Naw, same old shit, although I got this new cutie working for me."

Ron's voice is scratchy, most likely from his habit of chain smoking while he was drinking. "Great tits, nice big ass, I get her to reach around for shit as much as possible."

"You dirty old man," Paul jokes, grabbing his fresh drink.

"If they're old enough to crawl , they're in the right position," Ron sounds serious, but everyone knows he's joking.

"Wow." Paul takes a drink, then puts the glass back on the bar and sits on a stool for the time being.

Both men stare blankly at the television above the bar. It's the world poker tour and the players just hit the flop. The players sit emotionless, all with sunglasses on, shuffling their chips – pretty exciting stuff.

Paul slips his shoe off his left foot where no one can see and rubs his ankle. It was hurting worse and worse, the drinking really wasn't helping as much as it used to. The pain almost felt as if someone was stabbing his foot with a knife. "Mmmmm." Paul lets out a small groan as he rubs his foot for a second or two, and then places his shoe back on so no one notices. He finishes his drink in one big swish of the glass.

"Another one?" Jeb asks without even looking up from behind the bar.

"Maybe in a minute." Paul doesn't want to get too drunk. He is horny and would go home with any girl that showed him any attention.

Games Without Frontiers

Unfortunately there aren't any single ladies in the bar tonight, but that didn't stop him from hoping anyway. "Ron, I got to ask you something?"

"What's on your mind?" Ron turns to Paul from the end of the bar, and Paul walks closer to where he's sitting.

"Hey, I remember you saying something about getting a girl around here." Paul speaks very discreetly to not let anyone else know his business.

"Oh yeah, you wanna get you a little honey for the night?" Ron smiles to make the two of them seem as though they were partners in crime. "Here, I'll get you her number." Ron reaches to his wallet, pulls it out, and shuffles through some business cards. He finds what he's looking for and hands a card with a number on it to Paul. "Here this is a good one. Her names Dagny. She'll do whatever you want."

Paul accepts the card from Ron. He looks down at the card; it's nothing more than a business card for Ron's cleaners, The Wishy Wash, but on the back – written in pen, not printed – is "Dagny" and a number. Paul places the card into his own wallet and tells Ron, "Thanks."

"Anything you want," Ron repeats, and the thought of Ron having sex goes through Paul's mind.

"Yeah, I'll have one more, Jeb." Paul orders a last drink then walks over to the pay phone. He puts quarters into the machine and dials the number on the card.

"Hello," says a woman's voice on the other end, soft and somewhat cheerful.

"Umm, yes, I was calling looking for Dagny." Paul is a little hesitant in his voice when he speaks.

"Hi, this is her. You looking for a date?" Dagny replies on the other end of the phone. "I can meet you at a hotel."

"Umm, yeah. I guess the motel six by the interstate. Is that okay?" Paul asks very politely.

"Leave a rose sticking out of the front door of the room. I'll see it and know where to come, okay?"

"Okay."

"I'll be there in one hour. See ya then."

Paul hangs up the phone and walks back over to the bar. He finishes his last drink and pays his tab.

"Any luck?" Ron asks with a big shit-eating grin on his face.

"Oh yeah, I gotta run. Can you give me a lift by any chance?"

"Sure. Hey, I'll be right back Jeb. I'm gonna run with Paul somewhere." As Ron takes a few steps back, he loses his balance a little.

"Are you sure you're okay, Ron?" Jeb asks from behind the bar.

"Oh yeah, my foot just fell asleep." Ron plays it off to the best of his abilities and stands up straight. Ron and Paul leave together. Ron swerves all over the road on the way there.

Games Without Frontiers

Luckily, there isn't any traffic. They stop at a liquor store on the way. Ron buys some whiskey, and Paul buys a half gallon of vodka to take with him into the hotel room. Ron insists on drinking from the whiskey bottle as he drives down the road, and Paul doesn't say anything because he doesn't want to piss Ron off. Paul leaves his vodka in the brown sack un-opened. As they near the hotel, Paul notices a grocery store and asks Ron to drop him off at the store instead.

"You have to get a rose, huh?" Ron is being a jerk and laughing about it. "Sure thing, buddy."

Ron drops Paul off at the store, so he heads inside and buys a rose. Paul holds his sack of booze tightly in the paper bag as he walks through the store, trying to be inconspicuous. No one seems to care. Paul buys his rose and walks across the street to the hotel. He gets a hotel room for the night and leaves the rose sticking out of the doorway. Paul turns on the television while he waits and then grabs an empty glass and pours a glass of straight vodka, thinking to himself, *I should have gotten something to mix it with.*

Paul looks over at the hotel room clock; it's just about time for Dagny to arrive.

So Paul fast walks out of his room quickly to the soda machine, buys some Diet Cokes, and is back in the room in no time. He fills another glass with the Diet Coke and alternates drinking from each glass as he waits patiently.

Paul walks to the window of the hotel room and peeks out to see if Dagny is there yet. Paul doesn't have any idea what to expect, and now he is starting to regret his decision of calling a prostitute. He takes large swigs out of the vodka bottle instead of using the glass. Hopefully it will give him some liquid courage, because Paul is feeling very nervous about the whole situation.

Finally, a knock at the door. Paul walks to the door and opens it.

Dagny stands there, with the rose in her hands, and smiles. "Well, hello, I'm Dagny." She steps inside.

"Hi, I'm Paul." Paul closes the door behind Dagny as she enters.

"Paul, could you please put the money on the table there," Dagny says, sounding very professional. She's probably in her early thirties and not as bad looking as Paul was imagining. Her hair is red and curly and actually looks natural. She has piercing blue eyes, and her skin is burnt looking, as if she suntanned too much so it is no longer skin but leather. Dagny is wearing a small, tight black dress, which looks easy to slip on and off. She looks trashy, but in a good way.

"Umm, I'm sorry. I don't know what it costs," Paul stutters a little nervously.

"Oh, sorry sweetie."

Games Without Frontiers

Dagny turns and sits on the edge of the bed. She pulls a cigarette out of her purse and lights it. "Fifty is for everything."

Paul gets the money together and places it on the table.

"Now I want to lay down some ground rules." Dagny puts her cigarette down for a moment. "First of all, no punching or hitting; I can't walk around with any scars. Next, when you come, don't aim for my hair. My face is fine, or my tits."

Paul almost laughs out loud in amazement at her bluntness. "Okay," Paul agrees to her terms.

"So, now, I'm gonna make you feel good." She begins unbuckling his pants. As soon as they are off, she starts giving Paul head. Dagny goes at it for a few minutes, then stops, looks up and asks, "Are you too drunk to get it up?"

"I don't know. I'm really nervous." Paul is embarrassed and pulls Dagny up from her knees gently. "I guess, I thought this was what I wanted."

"Paul, I'm here for sex, that's all." Dagny sits on the bed again. "That's all the money includes."

"How long do you usually stay with someone?" Paul asks, hoping she won't get upset.

"A client?" she answers with a question.

"Yeah."

"I don't know, half an hour, I guess." Dagny seems a little pleased that Paul is actually taking a little interest in her.

"Well, I just don't ... I guess I didn't want to be alone. I thought I was horny, but honestly now I think I just was ... lonely."

"Look, Paul, I'm not a therapist."

"I know. It's just, if you could just stay for a while, you know, just talk to me for a little while, I'll pay you for your time – and you can have a drink if you want."

"Paul, I understand that you're being nice, but I really don't know how ..." Dagny looks around the room, and since it's a very non-threatening environment she says, "I guess I could stay for a little while."

Dagny stays apprehensive as to the nature of the business she's in, but somehow manages to get comfortable in the uneasy situation. The thought that someone is actually interested in her and not in sex is actually a little flattering.

"Thank you. Do you want a drink?"

"I guess. What are you drinking?"

"I have some vodka, and I bought some Diet Coke to drink with it."

"Ugh, I hate Diet Coke. Where's the vodka?"

Paul pours Dagny a glass of straight vodka and then hands it to her. "Thank you." She takes a small sip of the drink then asks, "So, Paul, I have a question. I hate to ask you this, but do I know you from somewhere? You seem so familiar for some reason?"

"Not sure. I was on the TV a lot, a while back."

"Why?"

"I killed somebody."

Dagny looks a little frightened when Paul says this. She asks, "Who did you kill?"

"Oh, just some asshole."

"Did you go to jail?"

"No, but I got a medal."

"Oh god, you're not a police officer are you?" Dagny looks as though she's about to bolt out the door.

"No, I'm not a fucking cop. I was in the military."

"So you got a medal for killing someone?"

"Yep, the Medal of Honor in fact."

"Wow, you got a medal, huh?"

"I did have some metals, but I pawned them for some money."

"Why?"

"Seemed like the thing to do at the time. I really don't want to talk about that."

"Okay, what do you want to talk about?" Dagny continues to sip her drink.

Paul sits next to her on the bed and gets comfortable lying on his back, now speaking to the ceiling when he talks. "So Dagny, is that your real name?"

"Yeah. Well, kinda; it's my middle name." Dagny stops herself from going on. "I really shouldn't be telling you this."

"Dagny, I really just wanted to have someone here tonight, that's all. I'm not going to go around telling anyone about this. I have to hire people just to have a conversation." Paul looks down a little, ashamed in himself.

"Well, I don't know much, but I'll try to talk to you." Dagny seems saddened by her own comment.

"Where did you get a name like Dagny?"

"My mother was from East Germany. She left there when she got pregnant with me." Dagny takes another small sip of vodka. "She read a book that was, like, illegal or something, and that's what made her change her mind about living there. She didn't want to have a child there, so she came here."

"What book?"

"I can't remember the name of it, but the main character's name was Dagny, and that's who she named me after."

"Oh, so you're named after a character in a book?"

"Aren't we all, Paul?" She puts heavy emphasis on his name. "I mean, isn't there a big black book where your name is an important character?"

"Yeah, I guess you got me on that one."

"Everything always has some reason behind it. You don't know why your parents named you Paul?"

"They told me once, but I don't remember what they said." Paul walks to the bottle of vodka.

Games Without Frontiers

He pours himself another glass and mixes it with some Diet Coke. "I have to mix this stuff up or it'll taste bad."

"Oh, okay." Dagny smiles. "I just don't drink any Coke products."

"That's strange. Why?"

"Ummm, when I was growing up here, my mother used to tell me about Fanta Orange and how that was an illegal way of selling Germans Coke."

"How do you mean?"

"Coke changed their name to Fanta so they could still trade products with the Nazis and make a profit.

All of Germany was so ashamed of the war that they even made a public apology, so it angered my mother when Coke continued to sell Fanta and prosper without ever taking any blame. So I have it embedded in my head not to drink Coke."

"Wow, you learn something new every day. That's kinda bullshit. I can see why your mother was angry."

"Well, you can't go around you entire life blaming others and not making solutions. I mean, I do what I do 'cause I like the money and it's pretty easy. I was never proud like my mother."

"That's one way to look at it. I just feel so unappreciated with the way my life is going."

"So you think that getting drunk and having sex is the answer?"

Dagny asks, knowing that she is being brutal but feeling a lot more at ease in the room now. "Paul, this isn't the answer you're looking for. I can tell you that – unless your goal is to wither away and die."

"I'm not sure who I am anymore or what I want." Paul looks at Dagny, who is now lying conformtably next to him.

"Well, it's never too late to turn it all around."

They talk for a while longer, and eventually both doze off. When Paul wakes up, Dagny is gone. He wallows out of the bed and walks to the hotel room door to lock it. He notices that there's money on the side table and a note. He picks up the note. All it says is "thanks". Paul puts the fifty dollars lying next to the note back in his wallet. Then he slips under the sheets and goes back to sleep.

28.

May 10's

Ben drives down the freeway fast, because he is running late for a charity event. He scheduled this thing last minute and still didn't know all the details except for the fact that it was important for him to be there, and it would be a huge tax write off at the end of the year.

Ben is dressed in khakis and a polo shirt for the charity event. He drives his brand new Camaro; it was part of the deal that he got to keep the car for playing the part of *Qaudren Steel*. The movie was still in pre-production, but he got to drive around in his souped-up Camaro as much as he wanted. On top of that, Ben got to keep the car after filming was over. He loved the car mostly because it was nice and didn't draw tons of attention, like some other cars would. When he drove around, Ben didn't really worry about people being too distracted by his ride. Also it was in his contract that he was supposed to drive the Camaro to any public events, which included charities.

Trying to dodge traffic isn't too difficult, so Ben dials his publicist Phil on the phone inside the car to get some last-minute details. The automized woman's voice comes on the speakers and asks, "Name please."

"Phil." Ben sounds as clear as he can.

"One moment please," the voice echoes, and then he hears the sound of a phone ringing.

"This is Phillip," Phil's voice echoes throughout the car.

"Hey, Phil. Its Ben."

"Hey, money. What's going on? You at the event yet?"

"No, I'm on my way. What is this again? Some kind of classic deal?"

"It's just a charity golf event. No big deal. Just have some fun and get on camera, and at the end of the day tell them your chosen charity, and they'll send the donation off from you. You'll be out of there before the evening. Cool, my friend?"

"Yeah, that's great. I don't have any golf clubs though."

"That's okay. They'll take care of you when you get there. I promise."

"All right, I'll be there in a minute. I'll talk to you later"

"Later bro."

The music comes back on in the car, and Ben keeps speeding down the road. He's not too far out now. When he pulls up to the club house, a valet runs to take his car and gives him a ticket.

Games Without Frontiers

Ben walks inside the clubhouse and is greeted by a young lady who's one of the promoters of the event. She's a chipper red head wearing a cute little golf outfit that consists brown slacks and a blue polo shirt, and of course a silly little visor. On her chest is a name tag that says, "Hello, I'm Tammy."

"Hi Tammy. I'm here for the golf tournament today, but I'm not sure where I'm supposed to be going."

"Well, hello there." Tammy turns her attention to Ben with wide eyes and a million-dollar smile. "Yes, we're so glad you are here today. I'll show you to your locker room. It's right over here. Have you got your clubs yet?" Tammy points Ben in the right direction.

"Thanks, Tammy. No, I don't have my clubs, so do you have some I can, like, rent or buy maybe?"

"I will take care of all that. No worries, mate."

Ben is relieved as he enters the locker room and changes shoes. When he comes out of the locker room, an entire club set is sitting inside a brand new bag. Also, a young man named Doug, introduces himself as Ben's caddy for the day.

"How are you doing today, sir? I'm Doug." Doug picks up the golf bag and rests the strap on his shoulder. He shakes Ben's hand. "If you need anything, I will take care of it for you, sir."

"My dad's 'sir'; Ben's cool, man. I appreciate your help." Ben walks to the front of the club house.

Two other actors that Ben knows walk by and they wave at one another. Good to see some familiar faces around, and some other famous people. "Hey, George. Hey, Brad," Ben calls out to the men.

They turn and say, "Ben, how's it going?" then continue to walk off.

As Ben looks around some more at his surroundings, he notices that everyone is in groups of twos.

"So are we playing with partners today?" Ben asks Doug.

Doug responds with. "Umm, I only knew that I would be with you today, sir."

"We can go look at the player's list. Everyone is grouped with a partner already, I think."

Ben and Doug walk around for a minute trying to find a roster to see who his partner will be. While looking around, a girl with a microphone wearing a very nice dress and a guy with a camera approach Ben. It's obvious that she knows who he is and wants to get him on camera.

"Here is one of our celebrities playing here today." She steps closer with the microphone. "Ben, how are you feeling today? Ready for some golf?"

Ben turns on the charm. "Yeah, it's great to get out for a good cause. It makes it all so rewarding, knowing you're helping those who need it."

Games Without Frontiers

"Thank you. Good luck out there today." The reporter and camera guy start walking away to find someone else to get on camera.

"Thanks, guys." Ben gets back to finding out who he is partnered with for the tournament. After not too much searching, Ben runs into Tammy again, so he asks her. "Hey, Tammy, can you help me find out something?"

"Sure, what can I do for you?" Tammy shows her pearly whites with every spoken word.

"Ummm, I'm embarrassed. I'm so unprepared. Umm, do you know who I'm partnered with today?" Ben asks with a childlike tone.

"Yeah, you're with him." Tammy points to another golfer whose back is to them. "Hey, Paul! Here's Ben. He was looking for you too."

Ben's stomach drops and his eyes widen. Much to his disbelief, Paul turns around and walks towards him.

"Hey, Ben, it's been awhile." Paul walks up to Ben and shakes his hand.

Ben's hand feels motorized and shakes back without any hesitation, but he says absolutely nothing.

Tammy tells Ben. "We thought it would be fun to partner you two together as the war hero and the actor that played him in the movie. Exciting, right?"

"Yes. Paul, I wasn't expecting this. Just caught me a little off guard." Ben doesn't really know how to feel about all this, so he tries to make the best out of a potentially bad situation. "You ready to play some golf?"

The two start their game together and make it through the first three holes without so much as a word spoken between them. Ben keeps smiling and acting like he's having fun. Every time Paul tries to make small talk, Ben just smiles and agrees.

At the fifth hole, Paul takes his shot, and as he walks away, Ben notices that Paul is limping a lot more than before. Ben feels pity for Paul and eases up a bit. As they walk by one another, Paul deliberately stops Ben while they're alone, where no one can hear. "Look, man, I'm really sorry for the way I acted. I just kinda lost it for a while there. I feel really bad now."

Ben seems a little relieved by the statement and decides to not worry about Paul's behavior and enjoy the day. The two are back to being friends in no time. Ben cracks jokes about the other golfers, and Paul keeps doing his impression of Michael, the director of *The Pain Cabinet*, which makes them both burst into tears laughing.

At one point Ben ask Paul, "So how have you been?"

"Well, it was kinda rough for a while there, but I'm getting everything slowly back on track."

"That's good, man. I'm glad to see you're doing well."

"Yeah, you too. How is Hollywood? Still shallow as hell?"

Games Without Frontiers

"Well, it is what it is, and it's sure as hell paying the bills."

"Got anything new coming up?"

"Yeah, I just was in a movie *Syphon Graph*, and starting next month I'm going to be *Qaudren Steel*."

"Damn, that's great. Glad to hear things are still going good for you as well. I'll be honest with you, I have never really been into comics, but I bet that will be great."

It's a little strange that Paul is acting nice, but it's more than welcome compared to his crazy, erratic behavior when he was fucked up. The two finish their game in third to last place, which really doesn't matter because their donation will be exactly the same no matter where they placed. After finishing up the game, Ben heads back to the locker room, showers and changes clothes.

After he finishes, Ben goes to the front desk where the charity organizers are taking information. He runs into Paul again, also at the desk, who is hassling the organizer guy about something.

"Yes, I just want it to come to my home address. Then I'll take care of it from there." Paul is telling the young organizer guy where he wants his check sent.

Ben walks up from behind Paul.

"Hey, I don't have a charity yet for my check," Ben tells the organizer.

"Just send it to the same place that you send Paul's, all right?"

Paul sharply turns and smiles, caught a little off guard by Ben.

"Are you sure man?" Paul leans in closer to Ben and has him step aside from the desk for a moment. Then he whispers into Ben's ear. "I really need the money, so I'm just going to keep it. If you send me your check, it won't go to a donation. Please don't tell anyone what I'm doing."

Ben leans into Paul. "Take the money. Use it for something good." He walks back to the desk and tells the organizer, "Yeah, I want my check sent to the same address as Paul's."

"Will do, sir." The organizer shuffles through a little rolodex and finds Ben's mailing address and makes a note to change it to Paul's mailing address.

Ben pats Paul on the back. "Good luck, buddy. You should give me a call sometime and we'll hang out. I've got a new place that I'm negotiating to buy, and it's in Colorado – not too far then where you're from, right?"

"Wow, yeah, only a few hours. I might do that sometime. I don't even know how to begin to thank you for this."

Ben and Paul bid farewell to one another. Ben figured that he would never see Paul ever again. Ben gets back on with his day after the tournament and goes to meet with Krista for dinner. Not another thought of Paul ever crosses his mind.

29.

November 10's

Paul was now two years and seven months sober and literally turning his life back around for the better on a daily basis. He used the money from the golf tournament to put a down payment on a truck. He was now living in a small apartment, but hopefully not too much longer. Paul's job at Buck's dealership was going good as well. When Paul started at the dealership, Buck took out some huge billboard ads saying that Paul, the war hero, was now one of the sales associates. People buying cars would ask for him by name when they came in to shop, so Paul was doing well with his commission and making some nice money.

Finally, Paul was able to see a doctor about his foot. He was wearing special cushion shoes that helped immensely. The doctor talked to Paul about surgery, and Paul now had enough money to afford it.

Paul was getting Caleb every other weekend as well, and things between him and Erin had become very civil.

Buck, his new boss, took a special liking to Paul. He let Paul work the hours he wanted and constantly promoted the war hero factor to everyone.

The job was a cinch; Paul was a better bullshitter than he had imagined.

Today was Friday and Paul planned to knock off work early to pick up Caleb and spend the weekend with his son. Today was slow at the dealership anyway, so Paul heads out of his office. Paul is out the door in no time and already to his Chevy truck. He hops in and heads to Erin's.

When he pulls up to Erin's, Caleb runs outside as fast as he can. "Daddy! Daddy!"

Paul parks his truck in the driveway and gets out to greet Caleb with a big hug. Erin is also standing outside with a little backpack with Caleb's things.

"Hey, Paul," Erin says as she approaches the boys. "He's been so excited to see you all day."

"I've been excited to see him too." Paul looks down at Caleb. "High five." They slap hands. "You wanna go ahead and hop in the truck buddy?" Paul walks to the passenger side, opens the door and helps Caleb into his seat. Caleb hops up into the truck cab and Paul helps seatbelt him in.

"Here you go." Erin hands Paul a backpack with Caleb's things, and he places it into the bed of his truck.

Games Without Frontiers

"Thanks. How's everything going with you?" Paul politely asks.

"You know, good. I mean, you know, just hanging in there." There's a distinct sound of sadness in her voice.

"Thank you for letting me have him over the weekend." Paul tries to make her mood a little better.

"You know, sometimes, I miss you."

Erin looks down after she tells Paul this, and then looks back up with a small smile and what looks like a tear in her eye.

"I miss you too." Paul puts his hand on Erin's arm. "Maybe we could all get together – you, me, and Caleb – and you know, just the three of us sometime, maybe?"

"I would like that." Erin smiles.

"C'mon, Daddy, let's goooooo." Caleb bounces around in the truck.

"We'll talk about this later, but yeah, that sounds great." Paul likes this idea a lot. "I think we should talk later. The big guy doesn't want to wait on us a second longer," Paul tells Erin then walks back to the driver side and hops in.

"Bye, you guys. Have fun." Erin blows Caleb a kiss.

Caleb waves and says, "Bye, Mommy. I love you," even though only Paul can hear him.

"Hey, buddy, so what do you want to do today? It's a little late, but we can still do something if you want?"

"I wanna see the robot movie. It looks so good, Daddy."

"Robot movie? You mean *Transformers*?"

"Yeah, I love *Transformers*. I like the truck. He turns into a robot, and then back into a truck."

"Yeah, he does. Well, we can go see a movie if you want."

"Pleasssssse, can we see the robots?"

"If it's playing, sure we can see it." Paul drives to the movie theatre, parks his truck, then helps Caleb. They walk, holding hands, up to the theatre. Paul looks at the billboard to see what's playing.

"All right, there's the one where the dinosaurs come, and there's the one about the chipmunks. I don't see any Transformers playing."

"*Chipmunks*." Caleb can barely contain himself. They walk up to the ticket booth together.

"Hello, what can I get you?" the young usher girl asks.

"Two for the *Chipmunks*." Paul makes a two with his fingers and reaches for his wallet.

"*Chipmunks*, yes!" Caleb is so excited, Paul and the girl sneaker some laughs at him.

The boys enter the movie theatre and get some popcorn and a couple of soft drinks.

"Don't tell your mom I let you have coke," Paul tells Caleb when they get their treats.

Games Without Frontiers

They enter the theatre, which is nearly empty, and find some seats right in the middle. Paul and Caleb talk a little, but the previews start right after they sit, so everyone is now silent.

A few commercials play and then the trailers start. The first trailer is for some kid's movie, that doesn't hold Paul's attention much as he chumps down some popcorn and swigs his drink. The second trailer comes on and bam, there is Ben, right there on the screen with a mysterious voice narrating the trailer. "They tried to kill him, they tried to destroy his power, and they thought they had …" A moment or two goes by, and then: "They were wrong." Ben's fighting bad guys in a robotic suit that has all kinds of weapons. He stops for a few catch phrases such as, "I thought I ordered the soup, hot," and then beats the shit out of some bad guys.

The title *The Hard Fight* gleams across the screen, and Paul whispers into Caleb's ear. "You know that Daddy is friends with that guy, right?" Paul already knows the answer.

"Yeah, Dad, you told me." Caleb has only heard him mention this a hundred times. "Why don't you ever see him?"

"He's really busy making movies. I haven't seen him in a while." Paul turns his attention back to the screen, and they sit quietly for the rest of the movie. When it's over, they exit the theatre and walk back to the truck.

"That was the greatest movie ever!" Caleb exclaims.

Paul laughs a little and agrees. "Yeah, it was pretty good."

The boys head back to the apartment, turn on the television, and watch a little TV. Paul shows Caleb pictures of the house he wants to buy. Caleb loves it, because it has a big back yard. Paul makes a spaghetti dinner, while Caleb watches TV. and plays with his action figures.

The phone rings and Paul answers it, "Hello?"

"Hey, it's me," says Tiffany's voice on the other line.

"Hey, I'm here with my son. What's up?" Paul puts the phone on his shoulder while he continues to cook.

"I've got the night off. Can I come over?" Tiffany asks Paul.

"Sure, you can meet Caleb."

"All right. I'll be there in a bit, okay?"

"See ya then." Paul hangs up the phone and continues to cook.

"Daddy?" Caleb asks from the living room.

"Yes," Paul answers.

"Who was that?"

"Oh, that's just one of your dad's friends. She's going to come over. She wants to meet you."

Paul finishes the spaghetti and makes them both a plate. They eat around nine, which is late for Caleb. When they finish, Caleb takes a bath and gets ready for bed. It's around this time that Tiffany comes knocking on the door.

"Come in." Paul is busy helping Caleb get his pajamas on.

Tiffany enters the apartment and sits in the living room.

Games Without Frontiers

Paul brings Caleb back into the living room to meet her.

"This is one of Daddy's friends. Her name is Tiffany," Paul tells Caleb, who hangs around Paul's legs, looking around and being shy."You wanna tell her hi?"

Caleb waves but doesn't say anything to Tiffany. "Are you still gonna read me a story?"

Tiffany bends down a little and says, "Hi."

"Yeah, buddy, go ahead and get the book. I'll be right there."

Caleb dashes off to his bedroom. Paul tells Tiffany, "I just got to get him to bed, and then I'll be right out, okay?"

"Okay." Tiffany smiles and takes a seat in the living room.

Paul makes his way back to Caleb's room. He reads Caleb a story about turtles racing rabbits, and Caleb doesn't make it even halfway since he's so tired. Paul puts the book down and sneaks out of the room and closes the door silently behind him. He quietly tip toes away from Caleb's bedroom and back into the living room.

Just as he hits the corner of the hallway, Tiffany jumps from behind the wall and starts kissing Paul all over. She tells him, "How are you doing, baby? Or should I say daddy?" She kisses up and down his neck.

"Whoa, where did you come from?" Paul exclaims to the attack.

"I've been thinking about you all day." Tiffany starts unbuckling Paul's belt and sticks her hand down his pants.

Tiffany was a twenty-five year old waitress, who'd met Paul through work. He came to her restaurant often because it was right next to the dealership. She'd had a crush on him ever since she found out who he was and the things he had done. After hitting on each other a few times, they were now fucking on a regular basis.

Tiffany was younger, but she didn't act it at all. She was one of those girls who always dreamed big in high school, but now that she had been fucked over by so many different guys in so many different ways, her only goal in life was just to find some stability, which presented itself now that she and Paul were seeing one another.

They get right to it, right there in the living room, and just as things begin to get interesting the phone rings. No one answers it, and it goes to the message machine. "Hey, this is Paul, leave a message after the beat," then a loud beep.

"Hey, Paul. It's Enrickson. I got this number, and I know it's been a really long time ..."

"Holy shit." Paul darts to the phone and answers it. "Hello? Hello?"

"Hello," Enrickson responds on the other end of the line.

"Hey man, what's up. God, it's been years."

Paul is a little surprised by the phone call. "Jesus, man, how are you?"

"I'm doing good. I was looking you up, because you'll never guess what happened."

"What happened?" Paul is trying to focus on the call, and Tiffany has come over and started kissing him all over.

"He woke up." Enrickson's tone is strange. Paul can't tell what exactly he's saying.

"What. Who woke up?" Paul asks, confused.

"Parker. He came out of the coma. He's awake. The first thing he yelled out was 'friendly fire.'"

Paul drops the phone, and Tiffany can see the look on his face.

She asks in a very calm tone, "What's wrong, Paul?"

30.

January 10's

Ben had some time off between films and was spending the
majority of his time in California, with a few trips back and forth
from his new house in Colorado. Any excuse to go to the mountains
was a good excuse; it was his new home away from home. Hanging
around the house in the mountains was Ben's favorite thing to do; it
was remote and private. Krista was always there with him. She loved
the house as much as Ben did.

As soon as Ben bought it, Krista took over and started making
some major changes. Her craziest idea was to take the back living
room that faces out over the mountain and knock out the walls. She
wanted to put up a one-way glass so that at night they could look
over the mountain and enjoy the view.

There were carpenters and builders in and out of the house
quite a bit. This really didn't bother Ben; the place was so big, he
barely noticed. Christmas and New Years had just passed, and this
year the couple spent the holidays in the mountains.

Games Without Frontiers

It was the most romantic days of Ben's life. Realizing that he really never had known anyone else to any real extant, Ben found out that he and Krista had so much in common, and it made everything that much better.

They were in love, and they didn't give a shit who knew it.

The days in the mountains were flying by, which was a shame because Ben wanted them to never end. Krista would be leaving at the beginning of February for work on a television show, and Ben didn't really have much on the calendar till the summer, which he would spend in Madrid shooting *Forty Seconds*, a thriller in which he was the lead role. It would take up a good chunk of the rest of the year. Enjoying his time off and learning how to ski was just what Ben had in mind for the present time.

Today was unraveling at the usual pace. Ben woke up, and Krista was already up in the workout room. He joins her shortly after waking up and stretching. They were trying to motivate each other to work out by doing it together. Ben wasn't allowed to gain any weight for the new part unless it was muscle mass, and Krista didn't get jobs unless she worked out at least twice a day – that was the way she saw it.

Ben takes his sweet time getting up today and getting his workout clothes on. After about thirty minutes of debating, he hits the exercise room. Krista is on the elliptical machine going at her usual ungodly fast pace.

"Hey." Krista notices Ben and smiles, but does not flinch away from her workout.

"Howdy." Ben walks by Krista and sneaks a quick kiss.

"Sorry, I'm all nasty," Krista tells Ben under her breath.

Ben turns on his little charming smile and tells her, "I like nasty." Then Ben grabs a couple of twenty-five pound weights and starts stretching out.

There are two televisions in the workout room, one for each of them.

Krista is watching the news, and Ben turns on his television to *The Simpsons*. It was the "Mr. Plow" episode, one of Ben's favorite, so he lifts weights for a while taking small breaks between reps and increasing the weight each cycle. Ben had become something of a body builder now that he was a famous actor; nowadays, acting was so much more physical than just being a good actor. You had to be ready for the Olympics if you wanted a part that was worth a damn.

He was working out pretty hard and all of the sudden Krista starts shouting out his name. "Ben, baby, turn it to channel seven."

Ben changes the channel to seven and it says, "Breaking news report: was 'the Shot Heard Around the World' a hoax?" written in huge bold letters across the bottom of the screen.

Bill, the anchorman, is saying, "It's been years since the event, and now the American soldier who was shot on the rooftop that night, placing him in a coma."

Games Without Frontiers

"Has woke and is saying he pulled the trigger and shot the enemy, only to be shot by his own sergeant."

Ben's mouth drops wide open.

Krista finishes up on the machine and comes over to Ben, who is standing completely still in shock.

"They're saying that Paul shot him because he was going to turn him in on some drug charges. Can you believe this?" Krista is just as shocked about this as Ben.

Ben's a little confused and asks her, "What's going to happen to Paul?"

"I don't know; they haven't said what they're going to do about anything yet, or at least, I don't think they have." Krista leaves the workout room. "I'm gonna get a shower."

"'Kay, babe." Ben stands staring directly at the television as Krista leaves the workout room. Ben keeps watching, ignoring his workout. The story goes on to talk about Paul and this Parker guy, that was most likely shot by Paul after he killed Osama coming up the stairwell. The two men had been seen on the base arguing earlier that day. Parker had been in a coma for years from the gunshot wound, but now the more he came-to from the coma, the more things he was remembering.

Ben thinks to himself, *I knew that was why Paul couldn't remember it.*

The story continues saying that no formal charges have been brought yet, but if the evidence shows that Parker is telling the truth, charges will be issued immediately. The news report finishes, and Ben skips the rest of his workout because his mind is all over the place. He joins Krista in the shower for a quickie, which pleasantly surprises her. Then they have their all-fruit breakfast in the kitchen. Krista expects Ben to say something, but he keeps completely quiet about the situation. They eat together, and then Krista leaves for a run into town to do some grocery shopping.

With some time alone, Ben sits in front of the television, flipping through the channels and trying to find out more on what's going on. When he sees some pictures of Paul with the president being shown on a news channel, he leaves it there. The reporters are going into more details, saying that the accusations could be false and no one's making any formal charges against Paul.

Ben rolls his eyes, knowing that they have already destroyed Paul with these accusations.

Ben actually feels bad. This is not what he expected at all from someone whom he felt he knew so well. He is confused and a little unsure of what it all means. Even though it feels selfish to think about it, one thing was for sure: none of it would affect him in anyway. The movie was made, his career was hot, and nobody would be able to take any of that away from him because of this.

31.

March 10's

Today Paul was picking up Caleb and taking him to a family reunion. Most of Paul's family had never met Caleb or not seen Paul in a very long time. He was hesitant at first because of all the controversy surrounding him at the moment. He was trying to carry on as usual and act as though he wasn't worried, and that it was all lies and delusion from the accusers. Secretly, he was scared shitless, but he didn't want anyone to know that.

Paul had been experiencing enormous pain in his ankle all day. Paul backed out of the planned surgery last minute, thinking he might need the money for something else, so his foot only continued to get worse and worse; now the pain was nearly unbearable.

A half-empty bottle of whiskey rolls around on the floorboard of Paul's truck while he drives. Things had been getting better between Erin and him, until all the news started to spread. Now she was fighting him again for full custody of Caleb as he reeked of alcohol every time she saw him.

When Paul shows up, Erin is waiting with Caleb in the driveway. "Daddy," Caleb yells out.

Paul jumps out of the driver seat and grabs Caleb for a big hug. He picks Caleb up and puts him in the truck on the driver side. Erin walks closer to Paul but not too close.

"What time are you going to have him back?" Erin asks with no hesitation in her tone. "Not any later then six, okay?"

"Yeah, that's fine." Paul doesn't want to make this any worse than it already is by starting a fight. He starts back into the truck when Erin gets his attention one last time.

"Paul, is it true? I remember you talking about him. Just tell me is it true?"

Erin is very sad, and Paul can see it in her face. He dodges the question by hopping in the truck and starting the engine. Paul roll's down his window and ask's Erin. "Do you remember when you said no one could take this away from me?" Paul doesn't make eye contact while speaking to Erin, knowing that he is asking something that would upset her.

Erin looks up toward Paul, tears running down her face. "Paul, I never meant to…"

Paul backs out of the driveway quickly, without any hesitation. Erin stands alone in the driveway as they pull away.

"Why are you going so fast, Daddy?" Caleb asks very quietly.

"We're running late, so I'm hurrying, that's all."

Games Without Frontiers

Paul runs his hand through the hair on the back of Caleb's head. "Everyone is excited to see you."

"Are they really?" Caleb smiles with the question.

"Oh yeah, it's actually kind of a surprise that we're coming."

Paul turns his attention back to the road and driving the truck. "I think they will be happy to see us."

They drive for about a half an hour till they reach Paul's uncle's house, where the reunion is being held. There are cars everywhere. It takes some time to find a spot to park. He really doesn't want to park too far off, because that would mean a long distance for him to walk, which would be hell on his foot. After some searching, he finds a spot sorta close to the house and quickly grabs it.

Caleb and Paul exit the truck and make their way to the house. The back gate is open, and people are coming and going from that direction, so Paul takes Caleb's hand and leads him to the backyard. Paul is hoping today will go well and get back in good graces with his family, knowing that he might need some money and these would be the best people to ask. Caleb was going to be his ace up the sleeve in this desperate plea for help.

As he walks to the gate, a woman is walking out with a plastic cup in her hand, drinking from it, she holds the gate open as Paul and Caleb enter the party. Paul doesn't recognize this woman so he just nods and says, "Thank you," while they make their way around in the backyard.

There are a lot of people at the reunion – a lot more than Paul expected. Paul starts recognizing a few faces, but as people notice him, their attention is drawn completely on him and Caleb. People make eyes and whisper to one another as Paul makes his way around. Caleb isn't saying anything and is being very quiet.

Paul's brother Jonah sees him and comes his direction. When Jonah is within speaking distance, he asks rather loud," Hey, asshole, what are you doing here?" Jonah is a pretty stout guy and doesn't show any fear to his older brother.

"What do you mean? It's a family reunion. We're family." Paul holds back his anger for Caleb's sake. Caleb looks back and forth between Paul and Jonah. Paul lowers his voice even more and says," I didn't come to start trouble. I thought you might want to meet my son."

Jonah looks down at Caleb then back at Paul. "Oh, you brought your son, so that makes everything okay?"

Paul tries to reason. "Look, Jonah I know there are a lot of things going around about me …"

"Yeah, you could say that. We all know what you did. You're nothing to us anymore." Jonah holds his ground and gets right up into Paul's face. "Take your lying no good ass and your little rat and get the fuck outta here."

"Look, you don't talk like that in front of my son." Paul cover's Caleb's ears. "I don't know what you've heard, but—"

Games Without Frontiers

One of Paul's cousins yells out, "Kick his ass, Jonah."

Paul looks into the crowd, which has turned all its attention to the confrontation. When Paul looks back to Jonah, a fist comes across his cheek and nearly knocks him off his feet. Paul loses his grasp on Caleb, who stands alone, crying. One of Paul's aunts takes Caleb by the hand and pulls him off to the side.

Paul gets back to his feet and yells, "Is that all you got, pussy?"

Jonah takes another swing at Paul, but Paul dodges the hit and gets a good upper cut into his brother's lower chest. Jonah gasps for air and loses his stance. As Jonah staggers a bit, Paul opens up with the front and hits Jonah in the head and neck until Jonah falls straight to the ground.

By this time, Paul's father runs into the middle of the fighting siblings with both hands in the air.

"Stop this," Paul's father yells out. "Stop this right now."

Paul backs away from his brother and turns his attention to his father. "He started it. I was just—" Paul can barely breathe between words.

Paul's father doesn't let Paul finish. "Just go," he tells Paul. "Just leave."

"Dad, this isn't—"

Paul's father interrupts again. "Don't call me that."

Paul is so ashamed by this comment he finds Caleb in the crowd and grabs him by the hand, making his way back to his truck.

Caleb is still crying.

Paul doesn't really know what to say, other than, "I'm sorry you saw that. I'm so sorry."

Caleb keeps crying and wipes his eyes. "Daddy, can I just go home to mommy now?" he asks through his tears.

"You just want to go home?" Paul asks in a very calm way and looks down to Caleb.

"Please, Daddy," Caleb says in a soft sweet voice.

"Okay." Paul looks down and forces a smile. "I'll take you home."

Paul turns the truck back on to the path to Erin's. Caleb finally gets a hold of his crying and sits in his seat, quietly.

Caleb looks up after sitting there for a few minutes. "Daddy, why does everyone saying bad things about you?"

Paul takes a deep breath and pulls over to the side of the road. He turns off the engine, giving Caleb all his attention.

"Who is everyone, and what are they saying?"

Caleb looks down at his feet. "I don't know."

"Well, Caleb, everyone thinks Daddy did something that he didn't, and now they're mad at me."

"But if you didn't do it, why are they so mad?"

"They're all confused, but it's going to get better," Paul lies. "I promise." Paul pats Caleb on the back of the head gently and says, "Just know, whatever happens, just know that I love you."

Games Without Frontiers

Caleb looks up. "I love you too, Daddy."

Paul leans down and hugs Caleb firmly and kisses him on the head. They eventually make it back to Erin's. Paul honks his horn as he pulls into the driveway. Caleb hops out and runs into the house. Erin meet's Caleb at the front door. She bends down and can tell Caleb has been crying, and with a fierce jolting look she turns her attention to Paul.

He doesn't wait to see what she'll do next. He flies back down the road. He picks up the bottle of whiskey from behind the seat and swigs it uncontrollably while flying down the road.

Paul makes it home. When he walks into the apartment, he sees two messages on the voice machine. He presses play.

It's Tiffanies voice. "Paul, stop calling me or I'm going to get a restraining order."

The next message plays. "This is Captain Willis. We will need you to come in around—" Paul deletes the message.

Paul goes to the bedroom, grabs some clothes, and throws them into a bag. He grabs a bunch of loose money from the night stand and then heads into the kitchen. Paul looks through a bucket in one of the cabinets that holds random numbers and addresses. Paul grabs the one he is looking for and heads out of the front door, never to look back.

32.

March 10's

The Confrontation

    This was Ben's last week in the mountains, and so far it was the most quiet. Krista is off working on a television show, and the construction workers have gone now that the "glass" living room was completed. It is a little lonely in the house, but nice to have a little time alone. The snow is drying up, and everything is quiet as usual.

    Ben finishes his workout and weighs himself: one ninety-eight; this is good, because Ben is trying to put on muscle mass for his next role in *Forty Seconds*. He'll be leaving the mountains next week for Madrid for three months of shooting. He wasn't really looking forward to it, but the twenty-million plus they were paying him was hard to turn down.

    Today was going to be somewhat casual.

Games Without Frontiers

Ben planned on knocking out his entire workout early. Then maybe he would make some dinner and watch some movies.

It had been years since Ben had sat alone watching a movie, and was sure as hell going to enjoy it. Ben cleans up and goes to his study where he has shelves filled with over a thousand DVD's. He looks through his movies and grabs *The Return of the King, Equilibrium, Fight Club, 28 Days Later,* and *There Will Be Blood.* For some reason, those five titles just jumped out at him, but he had no idea which one to play first. He decides to get dinner going and throw one of the movies in the kitchen television. He grabs *There Will Be Blood,* takes it to the DVD player and inserts the disc.

The film plays while Ben whips up his salad with non-fat dressing to go with the piece of chicken he's grilling. Ben eats his salad while the chicken cooks, and right about the time he's finished chowing down the salad, the chicken is done. Ben eats on a bar stool sitting in the kitchen, facing the television. He doesn't plan on it, but he ends up watching the entire film on the bar stool.

Just about the time the movie is ending, the doorbell rings. Ben looks up in utter confusion. "Who the hell could that be?"

Ben places all the plates and pans in the dishwasher and then heads to the front door to see who is ringing the doorbell. Walking across the house to the front door takes a few minutes. Ben thinks to himself, man, *this fucking house is huge.* Then out of nowhere he starts singing to himself,

"My milkshake brings all the boys to the yard, and they're right, it's better than yours." Somehow the song is now stuck in his head, and that is all he thinks about till he opens the front door.

Ben unlocks the door, except for the chain lock, and peeks through the doorway to see who is standing on his front porch. Whoever it is, they better have a good excuse for coming by unannounced. He doesn't see anyone at first so he loudly yells, "Hello?"

Then from the side of the door, out from nowhere, Paul sticks his head out and yells, "Hey Ben," with a huge smile on his face.

Ben nearly falls backwards from fright. "Fuck me, man. You just scared the shit out of me!"

Paul looks down and back up. "I'm sorry. Hey, is there any way I could, like, talk to you."

"Yeah, sure." Ben closes the front door and undoes the chain lock, then opens the door wide open. "Come in."

Paul steps into the house and stands in the front hallway while Ben closes the front door and locks it.

"Fuck, Paul, what the hell are you doing all the way out here?"

"Oh, you know, I thought I would take you up on your offer." Paul smiles and opens his arms to give a hug.

Ben accepts the hug, but it weirds him out a bit. He thinks, *What the fuck is he doing here?*

"Which offer would that be?" Ben asks, trying his best to smile.

Games Without Frontiers

"You know, at the golf thing, you said you were moving out here, and I just looked you up." Paul shrugs, still smiling.

"But how did you get this address and know that I would be here?" Ben asks.

"I didn't." Paul begins to look around the house some. "This is really a nice place. Well, I didn't know you would be here, so I just took a shot at it."

"Paul, how in the world did you get this address. I mean, it's cool that you're here, but I don't want everyone knowing my business, if you know what I mean?" Ben paces behind Paul who continues to make his way around, studying the house and admiring it.

"The check that they sent me from the golf thing – this was the first address. They changed it to my address, but this address was still on the envelope. So I figured since you were buying a house here, this was that address." Paul smiles and continues to pace around the house. He looks at Ben. "Well, aren't you going to show me around?"

"Well, yeah sure." Ben smiles. He shows Paul around the house and leaves his favorite room to show last. As they approach the second living room, Ben tells Paul, "And this is my lounge slash office." Ben flips on the light and shows Paul the brand new all-glass room. The room is a spectacular design, very futuristic looking. "The glass is one way, so no one can see in."

Ben flips on some more lights and the entire porch and back yard illuminates in a carefully design fixture. "Isn't that something?"

"Wow, Ben, this place is amazing. I'm glad things are going well for you." Paul paces around the room checking it all out. "This is great. I bet it cost though."

"It was worth every penny." Ben smiles and has a seat on one of the three leather couches in front of the huge plasma television, just a few feet from the pool table. "Have a seat, Paul. What brings you up this way?"

"I really needed to talk to you. I'm really sorry to just show up like this, but I need your help and have no one else I can go to." Paul begs a little, but not too much.

"Paul, I really don't know how I can help you, but I'm sure there is something I can do." Ben looks around unsurely.

"Ben, could I get a drink?" Paul looks over Ben's shoulder at the bar in the corner. "Please?"

"Not on the wagon anymore, huh?" Ben stands and walks over to the bar. He grabs two bourbon glasses, cuts up some ice, and then asks," What are you drinking?"

"Scotch, if you've got it." Paul takes his jacket off and gets a little comfortable on the couch. "This place is really great."

"You want to hear some music?" Ben asks Paul while pouring some expensive scotch into a glass. He then takes a drink from his glass, and walks over to Paul to hand him his drink.

Games Without Frontiers

"Yeah, sure." Paul takes the glass of Scotch from Ben and drinks a big gulp, finishing the drink in one swig. Ben turns on the CD-player and hits random. Of all the songs in the world, "Voices Carry," by Til' Tuesday starts playing. Ben turns the volume to a level that they can hear it but still have a conversation.

Paul puts the glass of Scotch down and pulls out a small flask from inside his jacket pocket. He starts swigging it.

"Whoa, whoa, take it easy, killer," Ben jokes with Paul, but Paul gets a little pissed off by the remark.

"Killer, what the fuck is that supposed to mean?" Paul sternly asks Ben.

"You killed that drink really fast. I was just joking with you." Ben is completely apprehensive at this point, because he's still not a hundred percent sure why Paul is here. Paul doesn't seem amused one bit. He fakes a smile.

"So you remember when I helped you out with that audition for the movie?" Paul asks in a very caddy fashion.

"Umm, yeah, how could I ever forget? That was probably the greatest thing that has ever happened to me. Thank you, by the way." Ben is one hundred percent sincere.

"Mmm hmm." Paul pushes his cheeks up. "Yeah, so, I need your help now, man."

"What do you want me to do?" Ben looks around unsurely, trying to get to the bottom of this.

"I mean, of course I'll help you, but how exactly can I help you?"

"I need to get out of the country, so I was thinking maybe I could go with you to Madrid. I heard you were going there on a talk show. Then that's it; that's all I need." Paul is very anxious as he speaks. He takes another swig from his flask.

"To be honest with you, Paul, I don't really know anything about smuggling people in and out of the country. I mean, I saw *Maria Full of Grace*, but that's a different story." Ben tries to make a joke out of his explanation why he can't do this, but Paul isn't really listening.

"Anyways, maybe I could just be part of your entourage or whatever, one of those people who follow you around and kiss your ass."

Paul's plan sounds brilliant and makes total sense in his mind.

"Ummm, well, they're gonna check everyone's passports. I don't, like, own my own G five or anything. Paul, I'm really not the person to help you with all this you have in mind." Ben shrugs a little. "I'm an actor. I can play a human traffic smuggler, but I have no idea how to actually do it."

"Why is everything a fucking joke with you?" Paul's entire demeanor changes in an instant. "This is my life. I need your help. I helped you. Now it's your turn to help me."

Games Without Frontiers

"Paul, if you need money, it's not a problem. I can get you money. But all this other stuff you're talking about, I wouldn't know the first thing about. You need to get a grip on yourself." Ben walks over to Paul to pat him on the back in a gesture of kindness, but Paul shrugs his hand away.

"I need your help. Are you not fucking listening? I don't need fucking money." Paul is breathing heavily and slurring his words pretty bad at this point.

"Calm down, buddy. Look, I know there's something I can do, but it's not this. Why don't I hire you a really good lawyer, or maybe I can bail you out, but this whole smuggling idea isn't going to fly." Ben is trying to make Paul understand that this isn't going to happen.

"You know what, just fuck me man!" Paul stands and throws his hands in the air making his way to the bar. Paul helps himself to another full glass of Scotch. He drinks it like water. "I thought you could help me!"

"A man can't truly appreciate the situation until he's right in the middle of it." Ben says with no hesitation.

"That sounds familiar, for some reason." Paul gulps his drink. "Where did you hear that?"

"You said it." Ben stares straight at Paul. "Well, at least, you said you did in the book."

"I've never read the book. Hated the title." Paul takes another big gulp and helps himself to another glass. "I lived it."

"Did you?" Ben regrets saying it as it comes out of his mouth.

"What the fuck is that supposed to mean?" Paul stands straight with his eyes piercing directly at Ben. "Why did you fucking say that?"

"I'm on your side, Paul. Why all the hostility?"

"You're acting like this is some kind of fucking joke. It's pissing me off."

"I think everything pisses you off."

"Ben, Can you please be serious for a moment?"

"Paul, you come to my house out of nowhere – you show up and the first thing you want me to do is sneak you out of the country. I mean, what am I supposed to think about all this?"

"You're not supposed to think. You're supposed to help me. I'm asking for help. You owe me."

The second Paul tells Ben he "owes" him, something inside of Ben snaps. Ben looks directly at Paul. "How could you say that? I owe you? What exactly is it that I owe you, I wonder?"

"Well, first off, you wouldn't have any of this if it wasn't for me and what I did for you."

"What exactly is it you think you've done for me?"

Ben's entire demeanor is becoming much more hostile at this point.

"You wouldn't be anything if I hadn't pulled you out of that lunch room."

Games Without Frontiers

"Oh, so I suppose there was nothing else to it – not the fact that I could act, or that the producers liked me? And I know for a fact the only reason you did that was to piss them off, because you weren't getting your way. I mean, c'mon, Paul. You come to my house with all this bullshit, and you expect me to just take it?"

"Just admit it." Paul comes back around from the bar with another fresh drink. "You would be nothing without me."

"Is that what you want? Is that really what you want, for me to say that? I'll say it if it will make you happy. Is that what you want?"

"No, because it will be a fucking lie. That's all you do is fucking lie. Fucking actor, can't be yourself so you spend your life trying to be someone else."

"Oh, I'm the liar, huh. Well, last I heard, you're the one who's been doing some fibbing." Ben can't control himself. He is so pissed at this point, he is about to explode. "Why don't you just leave now before this gets ugly?"

"So you believe it, all this bullshit they're saying about me. You actually believe it." Paul laughs. "And you think I'm the dumb fuck."

"I believe it, because it's probably true. It all makes so much more sense now than it did when it was your version of what happened. Either way, what the fuck does it matter? All that's done, and there is no taking any of it back now. There are no second chances on this one."

"You have to help me, Ben. You owe it to me. Your life has been a cakewalk since you met me." Paul points at Ben then back to himself.

"Oh yeah, the Christmas I spent in the boot camp, or the hours upon hours of physical training, plus learning all your stupid fucking lines, yeah, it's all fake." Ben rolls his eyes. "Do you really expect me to help you while you continue to insult me."

"It doesn't matter what you think now, because you're an accomplice, no matter what."

Ben clinches his fist. "Oh, so you get yourself into some shit, and I am always somehow involved. Remember when you fucking raped that chick in front of me. You remember that shit?"

"Where did that come from? I didn't rape shit. She wanted it. She just played like she didn't."

"Do you even listen to yourself when you speak and how fucking stupid the things coming out of your mouth are?" Ben waits for an answer, and when there isn't one he continues. "Look maestro, I don't know if you're even on planet earth right now. You've been drinking like a fish since you got here. No telling how much you had before you were here."

"Why are you being such a fucking pussy?" Paul throws his glass to the ground in anger. It shatters everywhere.

"Oh, so what now. You gonna kick my ass?"

"Say one more thing about me like that, and ..."

Games Without Frontiers

"And what?"

"Look, I came here because I thought you were my friend. I don't know why you're so mad at me. I just need your help."

"Paul, are you so drunk that you forget the things you just said, not even five minutes ago?"

"Ben, are you such a fucking idiot that you have no idea what you're saying?" Paul launches himself at Ben. Ben steps out of the way, and Paul goes crashing to the ground.

He turns over looks at Ben and says. "Ha-ha, I bet you think that's pretty funny don't you?"

"Paul, I'm beginning to think that there is nothing I like about you. I mean, I always forced the friendship through all the crazy shit, and you know what? I'm tired of it. Tired of this shadow you think I am to you. You're not my mentor, you didn't teach me anything, and honestly I don't see how anyone believed a fucked up piece of shit like you could actually have done any of this. You know what the hardest part of playing you was?"

Paul gets back on his feet and comes towards Ben.

"The hardest part was having to act tough when I know what a pussy the guy I was playing really is."

Paul takes a swing at Ben. Ben pushes Paul's arm out of the way and slams the bottom of his hand into Paul's throat. Paul drops to the ground clinching his throat.

"You know that after all these movies I've done, I've learned a move or two. I would quit this shit while you're ahead."

Paul is on his knees, gasping for air. Ben turns to walk away.

Through his heavy breathing Paul manages to get out. "You want to know what happened over there?"

"I know what happened, Paul. I know more about you then you probably know about yourself. I've read everything about you, the misconduct towards other soldiers, the suspicion of drug trafficking, the fact that Parker was going to tell on you the very next day. You fucking shot him. You were on the roof alone, and you fucking shot your own guy. I mean, that's a hero if I've ever seen one. You know when I found out? I didn't say anything, but it was that fucking day you came to the set drunk. Oh hell, that was every fucking day, right? Naw, the day when you didn't know how you made that shot – the angle of it – and what you said didn't match. He killed them when they came out, and as he turned, you shot him in the back of the neck. When Parker dropped, he fired the last shots of his mag into your foot. I was sure of it then, and I'm damn sure of it now, Sergeant."

"I guess you got it all figured out don't you? If you've always known, why didn't you say anything?"

"The truth wasn't worth risking my career. It was a movie. It was fiction – it wasn't real. It was all make-believe from a bullshit story you made up."

Games Without Frontiers

"The only person you tried to kill was your own guy, and you couldn't even do that right. I mean, what does that say about you? You act as if the world owes you something. Well, I'll be the first one to tell you that no one is going to give you shit. You can't just sit around and expect things to happen to you. You don't just wait for them. If you want something bad enough, you have to grab it and not let it go. You never had a dream, did you?"

Paul looks down to the ground. "Yeah I had a dream, and now your living it."

"You expected everything to fall in place, which it did for a while, and now you're all pissed off because you're not going to get away with it any longer. I mean you had a pretty good run considering what a fucking asshole you are to everyone, and you know through it all you got your fucking wish. You're on all the channels again. Isn't that what you always wanted?"

"What about Caleb?" Paul stands up, catching his breath.

"Oh, so now you give a shit about your son – the one that you were just ready to abandon by jumping on a plane in a heartbeat? I'm sure you're real worried about him." Ben is watching Paul's every move. "I mean, you don't own up to anything. You act as everything happens to you and only you, and you think I'm the one with reality problems?"

"You're a fake, a fucking coward, too much of a pussy to finish the job."

Paul steps closer Ben, about to take a swing, but before he can do this Ben kicks the shit out of the Achilles heel of Paul's wounded foot.

Paul hits the deck in horrible pain. He clinches his ankle with both hands.

"Why don't you own up to something for a change and quit blaming everyone else?" Ben steps away from Paul who is lying on the floor rolling around in pain. "Here, I got a little treat for you, something that might make you happy."

Ben grabs the remote to the CD-player and presses some buttons and turns it to the song "Games Without Frontiers" on one of the discs and turns the volume all the way up. The speakers are shaking the glass they are so loud. "I know how much you love this song."

Ben hits the repeat button so the song will play over and over again.

Just before Ben leaves the room and goes to his bedroom, he tells Paul this one last thing in a very calm tone: "You don't even know who you are. You're a fake, a fucking joke. I owe you nothing." Ben locks the door after he enters the bedroom. He hops into his bed and tries to get some sleep.

The next morning, when Ben awakens, Paul is gone without a trace.

33.

March 10's

The Death

"Sir, could you please roll down the window?"

Paul wakes up and looks around in confusion for a moment.

"Sir, roll down the window." The police officer is shining the light right into Paul's eyes. Then the cop lowers his light, and Paul rolls down the window. "Paul?"

"Yeah." Paul isn't seeing anything while his eyes are still adjusting.

"Paul, it's me Miles. Holy shit, how long has it been?" Miles is actually excited for a moment, and forgets to play the tough cop. "Paul, how much have you drink? You reek."

"I dunno." Paul rubs his eyes and his forehead.

"What the hell are you doing all the way out here?"

Paul points at a marker in the road where there is a small tribute to Shelly Summers and a picture of her.

Written underneath the picture is the date she died. Paul speaks up.

"That's why I'm here. I had no idea where she was buried, but I knew this is where she crashed. I came to make amends to the dead."

"For fucks sake, Paul, you're lucky I found you. I can help you out. Come on, get out of the car. I'll move it, and then I'll give you a ride somewhere you can sober up."

"I came to pay my dues and own up for the things I've done." Paul staggers out of his truck that's parked halfway in the road, with the other half in the dirt. Miles guides him to the back of the truck and lets the bed down. "Sit here for a second while I call a tow truck."

"Whoa, whoa, I can't afford a tow truck," Paul slurs and leans, nearly falling off the back of the truck.

"Paul, you're in quite a mess man. There are multiple warrants out for your arrest. Holy shit, man, you can't do stupid shit like this."

"How long you been a cop, Miles?" Paul asks with his eyes closed.

"Right after you left. I joined the police academy. I guess you kind of inspired me to do something with my life, so that's what I did."

"I inspired you?" Paul laughs a little as he says this.

"Yeah, man, you were my bud. I mean, we were roommates."

Games Without Frontiers

"That's got to count for something." Miles calls into the dispatch. "The situation is under control – just an abandoned vehicle." And then he says, "I'm handling it."

"What about the camera in your car?" Paul points to the front of the patrol car.

"Oh, you don't have to worry about that. They only watch it if there's, like, a complaint or an issue with something. Just worry about you right now."

"Paul, I'm going to move your truck. Hop up."

Paul can barely stand, but he manages to walk over to the patrol car and sit on the hood. Miles moves the truck up further on the side of the road, and then hops out and walks back to Paul.

"You all right?" Miles asks.

"Hey, you wanna see a trick?" Paul holds up one of his hands.

"What are you talking about?"

"A trick, watch this." Paul lifts his hand up in the air. "You see my hand?"

"Yeah, I see it. Why?" Miles stands in front of Paul with his flashlight shining on Paul's hand. "What am I looking at? We don't have time for this shit."

Before Miles can finish his sentence, Paul blind sides him and tackles him to the ground. Paul manages to get Miles' side arm away from him.

"Paul, what the fuck are you doing?"

Paul staggers up with the stolen gun pointed at Miles. "I'm just going to take your car for a ride, roomie." Paul runs to the patrol car and hops in the front seat. The keys are in the ignition.

Miles stands up and runs to the driver side door. "Paul, what the fuck are you doing?"

Paul hits the gas and goes flying down the road at over ninety miles an hour. He pulls out his wallet, opens it and pulls out his only picture of Caleb. He wedges it on the dashboard. Paul looks around a minute, trying to figure out how to work the radio, until he finally finds some music. "Jesse's Girl" is playing. Paul turns it all the way up. "Oh I wish that I had Jesse's girl," Paul starts singing along to the music.

The sun is coming up and it's the early morning blue. No other patrol cars have spotted him yet, so Paul tells himself, "You can make it to the border. You can make it to the border." After a few more minutes of going more than a hundred miles per hour down the highway, a couple of highway patrol officers are now on his tail. After a few more minutes, there are nearly a dozen police cars behind him. Paul looks back at all the cars and yells, "Fucking aye. If this isn't the American dream, I don't know what is."

One of the highway patrol tries to p.i.t.(pursuit intervention technique) the stolen cop car, but fails and runs off to the side of the road. Voices over the dispatch radio are calling out things like, "Paul, don't do this," and "You're just making this worse."

Games Without Frontiers

About a half hour later, the cops manage to spike-strip the wheels of the stolen patrol car. Paul spins out of control, and when the car comes to a stop he sits there for a moment as the police surround him. He finds a pack of cigarettes in the glove box and helps himself to one. Paul lights the cigarette and takes slow drags, deciding what his next move will be while the police surround the vehicle.

These moments feel like hours. Paul looks down at the gun, and then picks it up, ejects the clip, and cocks it. He looks at himself in the rearview mirror. *If you gotta go, might as well be in the blaze of glory*, Paul thinks to himself. "I need to hurry my hangover's starting to kick in." He laughs to himself. Paul kisses his hand and touches Caleb's picture. "I'm sorry." Tears run down from his eyes. "I'm so sorry. This isn't what I wanted." Paul takes a deep breath as the cops approach closer to the car.

One comes right up to the driver window.

Yells are coming from every direction. "Put the gun down. Put the gun down. We will fire."

When they are close enough that Paul can see their faces by his window, Paul lifts the gun into the air. He points the gun directly at the cop and pulls the trigger, and dry fires the weapon.

Bullets shatter the entire car to pieces. Glass flies in from everywhere. The pain is so sudden and quick that it's too much to handle, so Paul feels nothing but the shock.

Breathing his last breaths, Paul stares at the picture of his son, which was the only reason he had to live. Paul knows he won't be able to fulfill any of his promises anymore.

His breaths come less often and not as deep; blood is splattered everywhere.

A light shines, gleaming through the bullet holes throughout the car. The light blinds Paul. He closes his eyes. It's a beautiful sunrise on the horizon, and Paul forces his eyes open one last time to see it. A few moments later, Paul stops breathing.

34.

Years later

The Meaning

Ben sits in the actor's studio with James, the host of the television show. Ben is appearing as the guest. The lights come up and James takes over. "And we are back. He's been a soldier, a spy, a comic book hero, and the man who stole the world. Ben, how did it happen that you first came to Hollywood?"

Ben smiles. "Well, I moved out here, and you know I kept getting evicted from all the places I lived 'cause I couldn't afford rent. I was so broke for the first few years, getting jobs here and there, working my way up the so-called ladder, you know."

James takes over with another question. "You were sleeping on the floor of a friend's apartment when you received the part of Sergeant James in *The Pain Cabinet*." The audience claps when James mentions the title of the movie.

"Yes, but it wasn't the floor; it was a pretty nice couch." Ben laughs and so does the audience.

"Sergeant James was your first starring role, a movie that went on to win best picture. How was it being a part of that project?"

"It was a dream come true. I mean, it all happened overnight practically, and it's been one hell of a ride since."

"During filming of *The Pain Cabinet* you became close to the real life character, didn't you?"

"Yes, we were friends." Ben smiles and looks down. "We became good friends."

"Years later, in a tragic turn of events, it was discovered that the story was in fact false?"

"Yeah, but I don't really like talking about that, because I really don't know how to feel about it."

"You saw him soon before he died, correct?"

"Yeah, it was at a Charity golf game. We had fun, and that happened to be the last time we ever spoke." Ben pauses for a moment then continues speaking. "If he hadn't done the things he did, I wouldn't be sitting here today."

"Next was *Syphon Graph*, the film where you happen to meet someone special."

"Yep, I met Krista on that one, and we've been together ever since."

"And I've heard you have some good news on the way?"

Games Without Frontiers

"Yep, this will be our third, so we decided to get married because the third one kinda sealed the deal." The audience laughs.

The interview continues with basic questions about all the projects Ben has been involved in.

He gives his usual answers and recites the same stories that everyone already knows. When they approach the end of the interview, James asks some very personal questions, the first being, "How do you feel as your life and film as an art?"

"It's amazing how a song or a piece of literature or even a silly little movie can really change someone's life. I hope that my work continues to be thought-provoking and entertaining, so people can have a little time away from their lives and escape to a whole new world. More than anything else, I feel humble. I appreciate everything and all the support I've been given throughout the years."

"What do you plan on doing in the future?"

"Whatever interests me and pays well." Ben laughs at the end of his answer.

"How does it feel to be a father?"

"I love my kids more than my own life, and I would do anything for them."

"Any advice for young actors struggling out there?"

"Everyone always says never give up and follow your dreams. I'd like to say that, but I think the best advice I can give, because it worked for me, is try to be good at more than one thing."

"Never rule anything out, and never ever under any circumstances burn your bridges. You never know who you might meet and make friends with."

"Any regrets?"

Ben thinks for a second then answers.

"Only one: a friend." Ben pauses for a moment. "Someone I could have helped and didn't."

"There is a movie in the works about the entire *Shot Heard Around the World* issue, and you will, in fact, be a character in the film?"

"Yes, a much younger and dumber me, that is." Ben laughs.

"Any idea who they should get to play you?"

"Oh man, who would be good as me. You wanna know how I honestly feel about that?"

"About being portrayed by someone else?"

"Yes."

James asks this one last question. "Who do you honestly feel would be a good you, who would do you justice?"

Ben pauses for a moment and then looks directly into the camera and shrugs. "Bogart. But I don't think he's available, tied up at Rasta Rick's or on the Sierra Mountains." The audience laughs.

"But honestly …" Ben looks down, and then back up to the camera with a little smile, and answers, "Who cares?"